The Secret Journal of Alexander Mackenzie

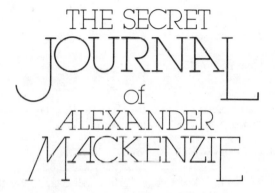

THE SECRET
JOURNAL
of
ALEXANDER
MACKENZIE

BRIAN FAWCETT

TALONBOOKS • VANCOUVER • 1985

copyright © 1985 Brian Fawcett

published with the assistance of the Canada Council

Talonbooks
201 / 1019 East Cordova Street
Vancouver
British Columbia V6A 1M8
Canada

This book was typeset in Plantin by Pièce de Résistance Graphics and
printed in Canada by Hignell Printing Ltd.

First printing: October 1985

The author wishes to acknowledge Cardiff, Alberta, where the idea of
this book was born; the Sweet Dreams Cafe, the Old Europa
Restaurant, Cafe Volare, the Blue Parrot (upper floor), El Cerrito;
also Neap Hoover, Jim Taylor, Norm Sibum, Nancy Boyd, readers;
Gary Fisher, interrogator. Some of these stories have appeared, in
somewhat different form, in the *Capilano Review* and *Canadian
Fiction Magazine*. "The Fate of White-Tailed Deer" won the 1985
Okanagan Fiction Prize.

Canadian Cataloguing in Publication Data

Fawcett, Brian, 1944-
  The secret journal of Alexander Mackenzie

  ISBN 0-88922-227-4

  I. Title.
PS8561.A93S42 1985   C813'.54   C85-091427-2
PR9199.3.F39S42 1985

For my father, who taught me to look at the world from odd angles, and for my mother, who taught me that there is always something to laugh about.

Contents

The Secret Journal of Alexander Mackenzie

Alexander Mackenzie was the first European to reach the Arctic and Pacific oceans by overland routes through North America. He embarked on both voyages from Fort Chipewyan in what is now northern Alberta, where he spent a number of years as factor and partner in the North West Company. His explorations, because they occurred in the less than flamboyant context of the Canadian fur trade, have received less attention than those of his contempories Cook and Vancouver, even though his achievements were perhaps the greater, since the hardships he endured were more extreme and the dangers he encountered at least equal.

The heretofore unknown journal that follows adds a new dimension to our understanding of Mackenzie and his travels. There is little doubt that it was written for personal reasons, that it was deliberately kept secret, and that it was meant to be kept from the arena of history. That it comes to public notice here and now is only by the sheerest chance, and that I am the one to reveal its existence is an extraordinary privilege.

There remains some question concerning its authenticity, but the same is true of all writings which purport to be those of Alexander Mackenzie. In fact, no documents exist that can be verified as having originated directly from Mackenzie's hand. The conventional account of his voyages, one in 1789 to the Arctic Ocean along the river that bears his name, and one to the Pacific Ocean in 1792-3, was published in 1801. But that document is generally agreed to have been ghost-written by a man named William Combe, using Mackenzie's field notes, some time after 1798. Similarly, Mackenzie's letters, the few that we have, are mainly copies of the originals made by his cousin Roderick. A fire in 1832 destroyed Avoch, Mackenzie's estate in Scotland, and obliterated his personal archive, including the letters.

The document that follows, because we have no originals with which to compare it, cannot therefore be absolutely authenticated. It was located in November 1962 in an antiquarian bookshop in Eastbourne, Sussex, England, written on sheets of extremely fragile paper tucked into the back pages of an almost equally fragile copy of the 1801 trade publication of Mackenzie's account of his two voyages. I received the book that same Christmas as a gift from a relative, and for two decades the volume sat on my bookshelf untouched, the sheaf of papers undiscovered.

About a year ago I was leafing through the volume, my interest in Mackenzie reawakened as a result of a personal research into the geographical region of the headwaters of the Peace River. A good portion of that region is now under water, and I became curious about what Mackenzie had seen there as the area's first European traveller. I picked the old volume from the shelf where it had sat for years, and the yellowed sheets promptly fell out.

There were eleven sheets in all, each written in a close but ragged handwriting. The ink had faded irregularly, and at first the writing seemed indecipherable. For several weeks they lay on my desk in full sunlight, undergoing the rapid deterioration common with old ink and paper suddenly exposed to light.

But while the sheets lay unprotected on my desk, I had an odd dream concerning an island near the mouth of the McGregor River, a principal tributary of the Fraser River near its headwaters. Mackenzie, or someone I imagined to be Mackenzie, appeared in the dream, shuffling around the island looking for something.

I'd visited that same island in the waking world some years ago, and I concluded that Mackenzie was looking for something that wasn't there. And, as sometimes happens in the logic of dreams, this error struck me as very significant. My curiosity about the sheets was piqued, and the next morning I rescued them.

I spent most of the day reading through the eleven sheets, as far as I could decipher them. They gave every evidence of having been written by Alexander Mackenzie himself, or were meant to appear that way. Over the next several days I compared the dates of the entries and their subject matter with the entries and subject matter of the 1801 journals. There was some discrepancy, naturally, in the treatment of events, but in the main the two texts coincided on dates and places. There were, however, a number of startling contradictions between this new journal and the published account, both in the chronology and the shape of events, particularly during the nine day period between June 10th and June 19th, 1793. And certainly the secret journal provided an altered perspective on the personality of this complex man.

The existing biographies of Alexander Mackenzie contain unresolved contradictions. Throughout his life, for instance, Mackenzie evinced a profound respect for European civilization and a deep affection for its comforts. Indeed, on the day after the initial entry of the secret journal, Mackenzie wrote the following to his cousin Roderick at Fort Chipewyan: "I begin to think it is the height of folly in a man to reside in a country of this kind, deprived of every comfort that can render life agreeable, especially when he has a competency to enjoy life in civilized society."

Mackenzie had already gained a reputation among his partners in the North West Company as a man who enjoyed strong drink and carousing, and later on in life his greatest pleasures were fine wines and the company of well born men and women, as indicated by his friendship with the Duke of Kent, among others. It is odd, therefore, that we tend of think of him as a rather unintellectual man, one driven by a crude and inarticulate mercantile ambition to explore, almost unerringly, the wildest and most brutalizing country in North America.

In those conventional biographies, Mackenzie is depicted as single-minded, sure-handed and decisive, as a courageous and

11

skilled leader of men—one who managed, through two long voyages of exploration, to lose not a single member of his crews to misadventure, disease, or violence. Indisputably he possessed those qualities in more than adequate measure. Yet it is also documented that he was subject to profound and probably clinical depressions, including one that assailed him in the year following his voyage to the Pacific, the period during which the secret journal, if it is authentic, was written or at least edited from field notes.

There are still other contradictions. After his voyage to the Arctic Ocean, Mackenzie took considerable trouble to improve his navigational instruments and personal skills with them. He travelled to London during the summer of 1791, ostensibly to acquire better instruments and to learn their correct use. Notwithstanding, he was at best an indifferent navigator and cartographer, prone to making careless and inaccurate calculations.

On the other hand, it is generally agreed that he was an extremely shrewd judge of human capacity and behaviour, and that he was a gifted ethnologist. But he was not a particularly sharp observer of any other aspect of the natural world, and he suffered from an apparent inability to delegate scientific or cartographic authority to his second-in-command. Nor does he seem to have been conscious of his shortcomings. Thus he missed many obvious and at times imporant landmarks in his travels. An illustration of this in the Pacific voyage is that he twice missed the juncture of the Nechalko and Fraser rivers. Whether he was sleeping in the canoe or depressed by the difficulty of preceeding events, no matter. That no other member of his crew noted to him this spectacular junction is mysterious.

Throughout his Pacific voyage at least, he seems to have been impervious to the intellectual propensities, capabilities, and judgements of his fellow-voyagers, particularly those of Alexander Mackay, who went on to a successful if ultimately tragic career as as a mercantile explorer himself.

Mackenzie took nine men with him on his voyage to the Pacific: Alexander Mackay, his second-in-command, Joseph Landry, Charles Ducette, François Beaulieux, Baptiste Bisson, François Courtois, Jacques Beauchamp, and two natives, one of whom carried the unlikely name of "Cancre". He rarely names any of his men in either of the journals, save Mackay, whom he seems to have regarded with a certain misgiving, and Cancre, with whom he developed a curious rapport during the course of the voyage.

Mackenzie's enemies and critics, particularly among his contemporaries or near-contemporaries, were numerous. His disquisitions with Alexander McTavish and Peter Pond, both of them senior partners in the North West Company, are a matter of public record. Simon Fraser, who a decade later explored and had named after him the river that Mackenzie was the first European to see, complained that Mackenzie's navigational calculations were often inaccurate, and that he exaggerated the difficulty of the country. He seems not to have noticed that Mackenzie traversed the roughest part of the country—the Arctic Divide—during high water, and that he, Fraser, passed the divide when the flood was past. And perhaps the final defence of Mackenzie is that he was in a hurry. Unlike those who followed in his footsteps, he had no idea of what lay before him. He did not want to winter on the Pacific, and the pace of his 1200-mile voyage was, even by modern standards, frankly astonishing

I believe that the eleven sheets I discovered are authentic; which is to say that they were written by Alexander Mackenzie, probably during the winter of 1793-94. The question of their authenticity is a matter of circumstantial judgement, one that is admittedly personal on my part. I believe they were written during the winter of 1793-94 because the sheets refer to no events outside their immediate concern, and because the text is singularly devoid of the hindsight and interpolation common to documents that have been edited or rewritten over a longer period.

As noted above, the events depicted in this new journal do not agree precisely with those in the 1801 text, but they do offer an explanation for some of the vagueness of detail in the 1801 text's coverage, particularly the vagueness over the crucial nine days between June 10th and June 19th. They also add some new information to the record concerning the apparent contradictions in Mackenzie's character.

Additionally, the entries in this new document are not characterized by the same style as the 1801 text. This may be in part a result of their fundamentally different subject bias and intended audience (there being no intended audience for this document). But I believe it indicates that the writer was a different person. Since the author of the 1801 text was not Mackenzie, the author of the secret journal, if it is not Mackenzie, can never be identified.

I make no claims either way concerning the quality of the prose, although I have taken the liberty of regularizing the writer's inconsistent spelling and punctuation and have added footnotes where I thought further explanation was in order.

The Journal Text

May 7, 1793

Tomorrow, or the day after it, having endured this harsh wintering of my expectations, I embark on a search for the route to the Pacific that will enable a linking up of inland and Pacific trade routes. I have only to write a last letter to Roderick, and send the six canoes to Fort Chipewyan with the winter's furs. The river cleared itself of ice almost a fortnight ago, and now the trees are brightened by small green leaves. The rills and uplands riot alike with fantastical blossoms of every shape and hue. While of little concern to me other than as signals of our impending departure, these botanic wonders seem to delight Mackay a great deal, his scientific bent more alert to these than to the responsibilities I set for him. He and the Cancre disappear each morning to hunt, and more often than not they return not with elk or buffalo, but with garlands of new blossoms, usually to the dismay and embarrassment of poor Cancre, for whom the display of skill in hunting, as with all native men, is a matter of extreme public honour.

Spring, in this wilderness, is a mixed blessing. The gnats and mosquitoes have returned with uncommon fury, and seem as eager to devour the flesh and blood of all the assembled human souls as the wild bees are to devour the nectar of the blossoms. And these clouds of buzzing pests pursue us Europeans with special vigour. It was these tormentors that awakened me this evening, together with the strange dream I had.

I have been in this country sixteen months since my sojourn

in London, and it seems more like sixteen years. The savagery and vacancy of this land troubles me since my return. My purpose in travelling to the land of my birth was businesslike. I sought to secure my place in the Company and to improve myself in navigation. Yet I found much more there than I sought. London was a storm of sensory pleasures, and also of philosophic disquisition and mercantile discomfits, the latter two centred around the recent uproar in the state of France. The merchants of Paris, it appears, have thrown out their King and intend to establish their own oligarchy over the French nation, usurping those born to privilege in favour of an elected republic. Which is to say, they intend to create a government in aid of their own kind.[1]

The implications of this turn I do not fully understand, but then, I think, nor does any Englishman. London was afoul with talk of liberty and what such liberties might enable for ambitious men. What took me broadsides was the manner by which most loyal Englishmen consoled themselves on this subject. The philosophic postures I heard men espouse bore no natural or logical relation to their positions or abilities. I ken that despite philosophy, the most of them will be governed by their loyalties to kith and kin, and to the Monarch. When their own assets are at stake, they will no doubt recognize little else in this radical turmoil other than personal danger and the possible deprivation of their social souls, and will declare the universe as it stands presently, in order and immutable.

A year amongst the savages of North America, white or native, I think would change their minds. Or a year in France, where everything alike is for the taking, save that there one must satisfy the newborn and capricious political soul before the riches can be garnered. Here one needs only the ambition, a body worthy of the rigours of the wilderness, and a strict governance of sexual appetite and violence, to succeed.

---

[1] The extent and identities of Mackenzie's acquaintances during his months in England are not known. Given his nature and circle of contacts, it is logical that he would have heard talk of the French Revolution. No mention of any of these ideas appears in the 1801, which, given the anti-republican shift that occurred between 1791 and 1798, isn't surprising.

Amongst my English acquaintances, all of them new to me, I held my tongue. The infectious tide of liberty, I think, is nothing but a passing illusion. Yet beneath it is a deeper, truer spirit, one that will sweep before it both idea and imperium. And with it dragging privilege, making strong men low and weak ones high. Power now and henceforth will be forced to stand more nakedly than before. It will not again hold sway without the glittering currency of constant victory and ruthless profit-taking. And I intend to lash myself to that glitter. Hence I have returned to Fort Chipewyan and this exploration.

I am not a man much given to the dream. That unwholesome part of the human soul I have tried to fill with my ambitions, and with the groans of my own labour. Thus, to have dreamed as I have done this evening disturbs me into this the morning's light. I confess that I have dreamed of a woman I encountered on the streets of London during a night of revels, one who temporarily unleashed my uncleanest appetites. I have not thought of her a whit since those days, yet here she stood before my mind's eye, fully transformed.

God in his wisdom alone knows why this matter opens here and now. I cannot clearly tell the subject of my dream—or dare not, save to say that if the dream be prophesy, this figure awaits me somewhere on the voyage ahead, and that she will be the source of my eternal frustration, and mayhaps, my salvation—at once a seeming liberty and succour, other else, decay of all that is decent and uplifting in this life.

May 13, 1793

We embarked on the evening of the 9th of May. I could not bear another night at Fort Fork and at midafternoon called in Mackay to stand prepared. An argument ensued, because several of my men entreated me one last night with their native spouses. This I could not countenance due to the increasing unreliability of the natives who are to accompany us. Amongst them only the lad named Cancre, who follows Mackay around as if that abstracted worthy were the deity himself, can be trusted. And indeed I have little sympathy for the lustful habits of my men. The Beaver women seem bent on any manner of debauchery with them in order that they stay on, the vileness of which is exceeded only by the filth of their persons. The native men themselves treat their women as little more than pack animals, and the grooming and general condition of these women is I suppose, due in part to the lacking in self-respect that comes with such treatment. My men treat the women somewhat better, yet I note that the differences between here and elsewhere are in degree only, not in custom, and my men respond accordingly, working the advantage of their paler skins and of the items they are able to pay out as bribes and gifts.[2]

Thus have my thoughts again twisted tonight to the woman in white, and the strange prophesy accorded to me. Despite this voyage is a matter wholly with men, I must take hold of myself and be watchful for the effect of womanliness throughout, I think. And such thoughts, in this wilderness, invoke a deep discomfit in me, both in mind and body.

As I sat meditating on these matters this evening, the lad Cancre approached me, announced it was his birthday and in the same speech informed me that the native guides taken from Fort Fork intended to depart our company that night under the cover of darkness.[3] I smilingly congratulated him on the anniversary of

---

[2]The apparent candour of Mackenzie's discussion of sex roles here and elsewhere in the journal is unusual for the period, and it may not be entirely in good faith. There is evidence, for instance, that Mackenzie did not govern his own sexual appetites with complete success. He is rumoured to have sired more than one Metis offspring while in North America, including one he is said to have sired somewhere during the Pacific voyage. Perhaps we should not be surprised by this—the history of Belles Lettres is full of moral self-admonition presenting itself as ethical and philosophical thunder.

In commenting on this passage and a similar one in the 1801 Journal, anthropologist G.A. Lockheed has pointed out that: "Mackenzie's statements on the role of women in Beaver Society are probably based on an inflated and paternalistic evaluation of the position of women in late eighteenth-century European society. He is almost certainly not comparing the status and treatment of European peasant women with that of Beaver women, which was essentially similar." (private correspondence)

[3]Fort Fork was a few miles west of the juncture of the Peace and Smokey rivers in northwestern Alberta. The site was so placed in order to exploit the termination point of an Indian trail leading into the Peace river area from the Lesser Slave Lake system. Mackenzie's maps show the trail as a Cree raiding trail, but in fact, the route was more probably used by the Indians for

his nativity, and took the latter information at its value and spoke sharply to the guides, telling them that such a course of action as they planned to commit would dishonour all their kin, reminding them of their leader's words concerning my authority with them, and of the glory of our task. I then called Mackay in and counselled him to put a close watch upon the natives, excepting the loyal Cancre. I also enquired of him how it came to Cancre that it was his birthday, pointing out that no man born in these wilds could possibly know his day of nativity. Mackay laughed roundly at this news, and when I remained stern, he told me of the interest Cancre took in everything about our ways. Pulling a slim volume from his coat and showing me its title, he told me Cancre had spent the winter demanding that he, Mackay, should read aloud to him at every opportunity, in the which he had complied willingly. The volume shown was of William Shakespeare's sonnets, the which I have knowledge of by my own studies.

•

May 16th, 1793

This morning along a glassy section of the river I was treated to several strange sights. The first was an island in midstream, some two hundred paces long, inhabited by a number of the huge Grisly Bears the natives so much fear. There were nine bears in all, full five of them newborn. My Canadians[4] immediately desired to shoot the beasts, but the natives expressed such horror and offence at their intention that I had my men forfend, even when one bear, vaster than the rest and covered across the back from neck to hindquarters by a swath of snow white fur, swam out

---

trade. The site was abandoned in the nineteenth century.

The number of native Indians Mackenzie took with him as guides and hunters is unclear in both journals. There appears to have been at least two at all times, and occasionally three, depending on where they were. Mackenzie seems to have left Fort Fork with two Beaver guides. Only one—Cancre—is ever honoured with a name or with an identity.

[4]Mackenzie uses this term to mean only the French Canadian or Métis courier de bois who travelled with him and who played a key if unhallowed role in the exploration of the Canadian West and in the fur trade generally.

into the river as if to intercept us. At this act on the part of the bear, however, Cancre stood up in the canoe and began to shout a strange incantation, one unlike anything I have ever heard, and the bear, as if affected by his sayings, turned back. It was only later that I realized that Cancre's chant had been in English, guttural and inaccurate as it was. This evening I asked Mackay if he understood Cancre's chant, and he replied with a smile that Cancre had been reciting the passages he has memorized of the Bard of Stratford.

The Grisly Bears, so aptly named, fill me with an unlikely terror I am loath to admit to. The natives say the sight of so many bears together, and on an island, is without precedent. And, they add, the adult bears were each female, and the white-backed bear the mother of all Grislys. I discount this as superstition, but am disquieted despite myself. Later on, I called Cancre to my side and, without mentioning my knowledge of his chant, questioned him concerning the bears and their habits. The Grislys, he said, once lived much as humans do, could walk upon their hind legs and talk and even still, unlike other bears, prefer the taste of flesh. But then, he said, they grew too violent, became solitary, and lost the power of speech. By his reckoning it was because the white-backed one still understood speech that he was able to turn her back with his chant.[5]

•

May 17, 1793

Stopped here this morning to repair the leaking canoe. Mackay goes off to cut bark, Cancre following like a dog, barking out his

---

[5]Native Indian attitudes toward bears, particularly toward grizzly bears, is a complex and well-documented subject in North American ethnology, and one that is too complex to go into here. Cancre's response to the sight of the grizzlies, while obviously not typical, is certainly not surprising. What is more atypical here is the proximity of so large a number of grizzly bears in one spot, since the bears are for the most part solitary, and the females, tending in particular to be solitary while rearing their young, are extraordinarily protective of their young and hostile to others of their own species during this period. Today, such a configuration of the animals would normally be logical only late in the season in parts of Alaska, during a salmon run.

fractured Shakespeare in broken accents. They return several hours later without the required bark, but carrying unusual blossoms they have located deep in the forest. The blossoms are nearly five inches across, and of a subtle purple hue, shaded almost grey. They appear fragile, and are soft as velvet, but these qualities are a deception, since they do not wilt and are sturdy under harsh handling. Each flower contains a bulbous core of bittersweet liquid that much excites young Cancre. He tells me that the liquid contains sacred properties the nature of which he is loath to disclose. I ate one of them at his urging, bulb and petals together, but found it not so pleasant as did he and Mackay.[6]

The Rocky Mountains appeared in the distance shortly after we again embarked, and their sight filled me with an ecstasy that quite overwhelmed me and brought me to tears. I began to think my pleasure at the sight an effect of the ingestion of Cancre's flowers, since he and Mackay seemed likewise affected by the sight. No matter. The sensation remained solely in my mind, with no accompanying bodily lassitude.

The uncrafted beauty of these lands produces an effect I have noted before, one that is somewhat painful to the soul. The civilized splendour of London, by contrast, was an unmitigated joy to me, each object marked by the labour of human mind and body, the alteration of crude materials and landscapes by worthy men. Here the beauty derives from an older source, an Eden descended to brutishness by the effect of time and inclement seasons. The uplands above this river, so filled with game of all variety that they seem a vast stockyard, are nonetheless sullied carelessly by dung and decaying corpses.[7] This surging stream, powerful

---

[6]The identity of this plant remains entirely mysterious. No plant found in the northwest bears any similarity to this description, with the possible exception of the wild rhododendron, the blossoms of which possess no hallucinogenic properties, and which in this locale would be far beyond their climatic range.

[7]Several anthropologists have argued against the accuracy of this description, which has a similar adjunct in the 1801 journal. They point out that the normal action of scavengers would preclude an abundance of carrion. Mackenzie may have viewed the plains mainly in the context of hunting, and in the company of his hunters, who generally hunted carelessly during this period in history. One also wonders if Mackenzie saw the London slums, with their open sewers and diseased populations. It is also possible that he was exaggerating here, unconsciously or consciously.

beyond the will of men, has cut its way through solid rock between vast mountains by sheer violence and the debris of its forcefulness lies everywhere, contradicting permanence. Thus the greatest beauty here becomes a decay and emptiness of things that seeks relentlessly an entrance to the human soul, wherein the will may be devoured. That I should defeat that emptiness within myself has sometimes, I think, been the impulse that has driven me to explorations. To have experienced it so coldly as I have done today fills me with foreboding. That I have dreamed now of the prophesying woman with her soft alluring speeches each and every night since leaving the Fork merely moves disquiet closer.

What can a womanliness of mind know or tell of this violent land? Should these wilds be one day civilized it will be by men of will and opportunity to whom all grace and soft arts will be nothing. A softness in the face of this, a sensitivity, can only offer up disaster. I must distrust all curiosity of things that does not run to opportunity of gain.

•

May 25, 1793

The men evince their distrust of my judgement, due to the disastrous traverse of the Great Canyon.[8] Several times in its early navigation I almost lost canoe and men before I gave it up to the cruel and late considered portage. Had I followed Cancre's judgement of the native route that moves beyond the canyon by a twelve mile traverse, all would be calm with them. And since their eating of the flower bulbs, Mackay and Cancre have been like as in a trance, and more like children than like men. Yet I detected in the sayings of the boy that no man of his tribe had seen this place,

---

[8]Peace River Canyon takes the form of a vast curve around Portage Mountain. It is now the site of the W.A.C. Bennett Dam, and the head of the 600 square mile Williston Lake. The dam was constructed in the early 1960s. Mackenzie does not exaggerate the graveness of his misjudgement. The 1801 journal documents fully that it occurred as a result of his distrust of the information provided him by his native guides, and that it nearly cost him his canoe and crew.

their informations predicated on the travels of the hostile Knisteneaux[9], who have travelled well beyond this spot. Yet, insisting on my judgement, I took my own course, and was near grievously in error.

Now after the precipitous portage we rest, putting the canoe once more in order, which has taken a terrible pounding because of my willfulness. It has rained heavily all day, and we are at the remnant of a camp made by marauding Knisteneaux, or someone else who employs an axe. While my men cut poles, and shaped new paddles, Mackay busied himself with the making of a cairn, to which I have attached a knife and sundry other items as a token of our goodwill to the natives who might pass here. To that store Cancre added a small stick chewed at one end to the form of a brush, that the natives use to remove the marrow from the bones of animals, burdening me with a lecture on the virtues of this substance in keeping of my health. Then he placed with the brush the last of his flower bulbs, the blossom yet unfurled.

Thankfully, I have been somewhat relieved of dreams these last seven days, mainly because I have been relieved, for the most part, of sleep itself.

•

May 30, 1793

The extreme cold of the weather continues to undermine our spirits, that and the ever darkening enclosure of the landscape. As I awoke this morning I recalled an odd dream that came to me in the night: a sensation of being far beneath the surface of

---

[9]'Knisteneaux' is the Ojibwa word for the Cree, who explored this area in the years before the arrival of Europeans. They were part of the general Northwesterly migration of Indians that preceded the arrival of Europeans across North America. The migration was occasioned by at least two factors: 1) the advent and circulation of the horse (probably through domestication of wild horses from Mexico), and guns, which together enabled North American Indians to successfully hunt and live on the Great Plains, and 2) the enforced later displacement of a number of forest Indian tribes from the eastern United States, most notably the Sioux and Cheyenne. The Cree must have been disappointed when they arrived in this wilderness (see notes 14 and 16).

a huge lake, yet labouring as normal atop our river, which travelled swiftly, as it tends to in these enclosed regions. Beside us along the banks were the drowned corpses of the great trees, and in the air around us swam diseased and ugly fish with enormous sucking mouths, poking through the rotting corpses of moose-deer, elk, and the great Grisly Bears. A vast unearthly drone invaded our ears from every side, making us all quite bewildered. From time to time one of the great trees would loosen from its moorage in the drowned rocks and shoot toward the surface of the water at astonishing velocity, breaking through the pall of debris that seemed to cover the surface of the lake far above me.

As our company embarked upon the river this morning, Mackay, greatly agitated, took me aside and spoke of a similar night experience, wondering aloud what it might mean. I kept my counsel, however, and told him it was no doubt the poisonous effects of the bulb-eating he and Cancre had indulged in, and that, their supply being exhausted, the illusion was temporary. We were interrupted in this discourse by the barking of our dog. He soon exposed a wolf, which had no doubt been drawn by smell of our fresh supply of meat. The beast followed us with its occasional eerie howls for several hours before it disappeared into the brooding stillness of the forest.[10]

•

June 4, 1793

The water rises constantly, often so abruptly that we camp above the river several feet and find our baggage surrounded and soaked through by morning. Since we have taken this southern fork[11]

---

[10]This sighting of a single wolf appears to be a curious counterpoint to the sighting of multiple grizzly bears in the journal entry for May 16. It is in fact not unusual. During this part of the season wolves are denning, and hence rarely travel in the packs popularly depicted.

[11]Mackenzie is now proceeding upstream on the Parsnip River, having chosen the southern fork at the juncture where the Findlay and Parsnip rivers once became the Peace (it is now under Williston Lake). Mackenzie made this choice on the advice of his native guides, even though the Findlay appeared to be the larger and more smooth of the two streams.

on the information of the natives and against my instinct and the wishes of my Canadians, I have been subject to fits of accidie,[12] the which I counter by feigning sleep. This is not difficult, since each man sleeps as he can with the hours of darkness only about four hours daily. I think we draw close to the very core and home of the continent's savagery. White-rushing streams burst from the banks without warning, and where the land levels itself and the river slows its rush is beaver muskeg, with the blackest beaver I have ever seen in thick abundance. But where such lands are, the air becomes so thick with sucking insects of sundry kinds, we are near driven mad. My mind is asunder from its natural habits and partitioned: the plenitude and coloration of the beaver bodes well for the trade, yet the distances and terrain militate against the gathering of large profits. And the mountains tower above us in cold serene magnificence, as if belittling our efforts. I found this morning several trees downed into the stream by the flood, so close by our passage that we heard the report of their demise as that from a musket. Had these trees come down as we passed, just a few minutes later, our ambitions would certainly be over.

Aside from the beaver we see little game beyond predators, and these seem almost to mock our humanity by their number. This, certainly, should never be a land for common habitation by men. What little evidence we find of native occupation is wretched indeed. And what degree of comfort is possible here? The sole release from discomfort and pain is in sleep, and thence, for me at least, to a different excruciation by lascivious dream.[13]

•

June 10, 1793

After considerable coaxing on our part we have achieved contact with a small band of natives. These persons, sickly and

---

[12]An archaic term with a complex meaning, popularly used until the nineteenth century by European intellectuals to describe a philosophically based desire to cease to exist. The last known use of the term occurrs in *The Unquiet Grave*, by Cyril Connolly (1945).

[13]They are probably in the vicinity of the mouth of the Pack River.

miserable in their material state beyond imagining, are of the lowest spirits amongst human kind I have seen on this continent, refugees from the great native migration that appears to have just preceded the coming of European men everywhere across the north.[14] There are some fifteen souls here, assembled: three men, three women to whom are mated the men in loose array, and eight children of undetermined gender. The last of the fifteen is a woman, older and by all degrees their leader. None of them have seen men like us before, although the older woman has heard tales of us, and of our implements, the which her people are eager to possess.

The men amongst them, with their urchins, take to Mackay, who questions them concerning his own interests. My own men, taking this as their cue, proceed to employ the women in the disgorging of their lusts, while the other woman, after bathing her body in the icy stream—an unusual practice in these regions—presents herself to me for like use, the which advantage I refuse, preferring to question her concerning the way beyond and other matters that

---

[14]"About 2000 years ago the climate across North Western North America deteriorated. This was marked by the southern spread of the boreal forest, and the disappearance of prairie-parkland and the attendant herds of bison and caribou. Native tool inventories became much less specialized, and the great variety of trade goods present in the archaeological record in Southwest Yukon, Southwest Mackenzie and Northeast British Columbia disappeared. The encroaching forest meant that people were much less mobile (travelling in a black spruce jungle is extremely difficult), and native populations became tied to the rabbit/lynx cycle. There was no buffer like the bison against the kind of cycle that rabbit and apparently moose populations are caught in. Without bison or salmon as an alternate source of food, human societies, in order to survive, must not increase beyond the minimum carrying capacity of the country they live in. This meant, for this region at least, minimal or seasonal human populations. Then, around the middle to the end of the eighteenth century, the Sekani were pushed west of the mountains by the Cree and Beaver Indians. Prior to that, the Sekani had wintered east of the mountains, living on the large herds of bison south of the Peace River. Now they had to spend from November until midsummer up in the mountain valleys hunting caribou, moose and goat. The fur trade further disrupted their culture, although they probably saw it as a buffer against starvation. But in order to take advantage of the rewards offered by the fur trade, the Sekani had to spend more time down in the river valleys where there was more snow and less game, but where the majority of the valuable fur-bearing animals were. This process actually further marginalized these and other Northern Athapaskans who didn't have access to salmon or bison" (note provided by G.A. Lockheed).

add to my understanding. This proves the worthier course despite that I found her attractive notwithstanding her age, which is probably little more than mine but seems greater given the rough use living has put her to.[15]

Upon questioning she swiftly reveals a different character than her bedraggled companions. I find that I can understand her language easily, and so send away Cancre, who has sat by to interpret. In this he declines, expressing a strong wish to listen to her speeches, the which, since I have only the same interest, I see no harm in the indulgence of. She informs me that I should not be deceived by the sad appearance of herself and her people. They are not, she professes, of such misery as to our eyes they shew. This is ludicrous pride, and I declare it so boldly, but her gaze stops my cynical mirth in mid-course.

By a devious path of words I may not duplicate here because I lack her arts, I am made to understand that these seeming outcasts from all that is comfortable have sought out this very region, in order that they be able to experience contemplative thought at its richest, which is to say, at the depth of circumstance and stress.[16] She speaks of a disease amongst human beings that

---

[15]This entire episode, which took place southwest of the old site of Anzac, is certainly atypical of Sekani behaviour. It should be noted that according to Diamond Jenness the lending of wives was not a Sekani custom, "...only their awe at the presence of the first white man made them complaisant in this respect towards the crew of Sir Alexander Mackenzie's canoe" (The Sekani Indians of B.C., 1937, p. 54).

The behaviour of the woman who attached herself to Mackenzie is also atypical. It may be that the woman is of a different tribal origin, or that she spent time with the Beaver or Cree, both of whose languages Mackenzie understood to some extent.

[16]These statements appear to be a questionable interpretation on the part of Mackenzie, and possibly based on an overestimation of his own skills with the languages involved. Given the marginality of Sekani life, materialism in the sense that Mackenzie has her speaking of was probably not even imaginable, particularly to those groups who didn't have access to salmon. The separation from the natural world that has blinded Europeans to the kinds of macroecological processes the woman (or Mackenzie) speaks of here was almost indisputably the result of agriculture. Athapaskans in the Arctic drainage certainly didn't have the arrogance of agriculturalists, but neither would they have so articulate a conceptual grasp of macroecology. G.A. Lockheed has suggested that the Sekani woman may be speaking about the possibility of a spirit quest, although this practice is usually an individual rather than group undertaking.

26

inculcates the thoughtless conviction that contemplation of the condition of the All is of secondary import, saying that a blind furtherance of material well-being for the individual body leads the intelligence of men into a great sickness, one that, going unchecked, will sap the vitality of the waters, skies and stones, and leave but barrenness and violence.

The alternate to this loss of capacity, says she, rests in the technique of yoking memory of a completed material realm to each active calculation on its parts, such that one's singular industries become materially lodged in, and qualified by, a consideration of wholeness. She then takes from her bodice a portion of exquisite deerskin, the thinness of which was not much beyond that of paper, yet had, upon my handling of it, the softness and tensile strength of the finest velour. Upon this skin she marks a series of symbols I could not comprehend, save that the constellation of them marks out the shape of a great hall, more or less circular, surrounding a small stage. I explain to her that my technique of memory differs, and to demonstrate my means I expose to her this journal, to which she in turn responds by taking it from my hands and wrapping it with her deerskin. I accept her gift, seeing that, tightly wrapped, it will withstand the invasions of the elements in superior fashion to the oilskin presently employed to protect it.

Yet I confess to an increasing irritation with her abstract talk, although Cancre sits as if transfixed, nodding his black head of hair at every sentence's commission. But by my pushing her ever to more practical subjects, at length she speaks about a lake that rests a few days' journey hence, beyond which the waters change their course and go in the opposite direction.[17] This news fills me with delight, but then her countenance darkens, and after a long silence, she portends of black water, swift and boiling, and of a danger that lies beyond it, the lineaments of which she refuses to, or cannot, elaborate. Then she mentions a wide river that runs toward the midday sun, and natives of extremely violent character we will meet there should we succeed in passing through the black

---

[17]Almost certainly Arctic Lake, near the headwaters of the Parsnip river.

27

waters. After these remarks, she falls silent, sitting before me still, and commences to low moans. I soon fall into a deep sleep, counselling her to remain nearby, thinking that her doing so will keep her from the rough uses of my men.

In awakening near to dawn I discover she is quite vanished the camp. The Cancre sleeps still, as if dead, and without wakening him I check the luggage for thefts but find only additions placed within, in the form of quantity of the bulbous flowers previously discovered and consumed by Cancre and Mackay. These are smaller and of somewhat darker hue, as befits the locale. No one amongst my men has seen her parting, since they are all occupied with their rounds of lust, or torpid on the ground. I determine to keep the bulbs from Mackay, and so I secret them within my luggage. My suspicion is that these flowers are of trade value, and might be of utility with the fierce natives said to dwell below here; I base my calculation on the fact that these people have acquired some measure of trade with them, despite the meagreness of their region and the culture they employ.

Mackay has meanwhile secured from the native men a crude map sketched out on bark with a piece of coal. This map confirms the high lake and the switching of the waters. His research through the night has likewise uncovered rumours of the westward flowing river but no exact knowledges of it are professed by his subjects.

By ten we are ready, having completed our trade, in which I am most generous to the natives out of respect for their sad condition. The woman has not reappeared, and no one amongst either party mentions her absence. Out of pity Cancre tries to leave his fowling piece with them, but discovering his plot I send him back to fetch it with dispatch.

•

June 12, 1793

A few miles above the native camp, the woman reappears to intercept us, carrying on her shoulders a small packet wrapped in the cured skin of moose-deer. Without mentioning her disappearance the night before, she confirms the accuracy of the map, and indicates her desire to accompany us to the juncture with the westerly-flowing river, where she says she has some manner of trade to conduct. Although the taking on of a woman is unorthodox, I agree to the procedure, bargaining with myself that I will learn more from her, and will be able to keep my men from misusing her person. In both of these I have calculated accurately. She has won the admiration of my men, being equally as strong despite her smaller stature, and she is literate concerning the narrow motions of the country.

Thus have we reached the high divide, whereon the waters turn to the south.[18] Our passage up to it was uneventful within the boundaries of our recent labours, although the levels of the flooding waters seem to rise by the hour. As we neared the dividing point, we traversed a small oblong lake running east by south, the waters clean and icy, but very still. Then up again some hundred paces and below us a little we can see another lake, similar save that the water of it is dark and bearded with a thick yellow scum, and exceedingly bitter to the taste according to Mackay, who climbed down to it for a closer observation of its peculiar condition.

We rest here while I take compass bearings and write these words in my journal, although the place is hardly beautiful to the eye, and is in no wise accommodating to leisure. The air is both rankled with chill winds and filled with insects. To the south runs a sharp ridge that follows up to a mountain into the southwest, and almost due east is another peak of equal stature. Down the westerly shore of the lake, which is so high in volume it overruns its shores and leaks into the forest wherever it can, boil two vigorous streams. Our canoe, already weakened, requires repairs before embarking, but there is little material available except that of spruce and liard.[19]

Mackay had been told by one of the natives to expect the

---

[18]This stretch of land, between Arctic and Pacific lakes, is one of the dividing points between the Arctic and Pacific drainage basins. Mackenzie's description of the spot is uncharacteristically careful and accurate.

[19]Liard is balsam fir, a softwood of low quality common in the region at medium to low elevations where the water table is moderately high.

company of more of their kin at this point, but this proves to be nothing but an idle boast, leading from the desire of the natives to please their guests. Upon his asking her the whereabouts of the promised persons, the woman informed Mackay that such practice is expected of a host, and that a guest should be told, in the absence of pleasing informations, those things that will produce a mental euphony. I have noted this practice elsewhere in the past, but without this understanding of its purpose, declared it then to be mere miscreant behaviour. The woman readily admitted to me that no such kin exist, and that indeed no native is so foolish as to travel on or at the flood, as we do. Only the usual signpost stockpiling of implements is here to greet us.[20] We add a little, and subtract items of practical interest, mainly those that promise aid in acquiring fish. There is little game to be had hereabouts, according to the woman, but at certain times there are trout in reasonable plenty.

I make a good show of my enthusiasm at this juncture, but feel nothing of it myself. At this, the dividing of the continent's waters, and at its savage rooftop, I experience only personal doubts and an unreasonable measure of terror. Indeed, I begin to wonder if I am to be taken apart by the native woman's dire prophecy, which, added to the one of the white-clad woman from my frequent nightmares, promises nothingness as the reward for all my efforts. Am I, as the native woman informs me, locked in the forestays of a stupendous error that will generate consequences for two hundred years or more before it is exposed?

My private ambitions, and according to her, those of the men who will follow me, will be to subdue, to exploit, to superimpose a civilized image by brute force upon this savage continent. At no foreseeable point will we stoop to consider the logic of the continent's own language and crude reality. It is true that I, as

---

[20]Caches of implements were often stored at fishing or hunting camps by a number of tribes, particularly where they were not deeply fearful of marauding invaders. In one respect, they were true caches, but in another, they were meant to display the high level of culture and technology of the locals to those passing through. Mackenzie made a habit of interfering with these caches, usually by removing items of artistic novelty or of practical use, and replacing them with iron implements or beads. In essence, he was leaving merchandise samples; advertising.

the first, am too conscious of time to slow my pace, too eager for possible profit and gain to seek out its genius and spirit. And those who follow, I fear, will do as I have done. These very thoughts unbalance me with their treason, as if a partition of my soul, if a soul I have, has been broken open against the remainder. I am thus almost enemy to my ambitions, and only the awkwardness of my situation here stays my will, which would fain heed this womanliness of mind and abandon the geographic fulcrum we have reached, and depart this place and continent forever.

•

June 14, 1793

On this day disaster overtakes us. Since entering the southeasterly lake and the stream that lay beyond it yesterday, the terrain has worsened steadily, closing in around the black and scum-ridden waters such that in some stretches our passage is walled by sheer rock and the river studded with boulders fallen from these walls. Where the hurrying waters and treacherous boulders do not threaten us, there are huge embarras[21] to block our passage, built of recently wrecked trees brought down by the flood.

This turn disheartens the men greatly, who have the expectation that, being more southerly here and now moving with the current, their load of work should ease. Instead, disaster threatens us minute by hour, yard by yard, argued back only by luck and our strong backs. By evening all are exhausted and chilled from having spent a goodly part of the hours leaping into and out of the icy waters to maintain the safety of our craft. Yet a dram of rum for each and my exhortations still their complaints. I sent Mackay a mile forward to search the river, and he and the Cancre returned with no news of relief. I call this stream the Bad River, because it has no equal in the production of danger and misery,

---

[21]'Embarra' is the term Mackenzie uses for jams created in the course of a stream by flood debris and deadfall. Anyone who knows that part of the country will testify that Mackenzie exaggerates nothing in his description of the size and dangerousness of these jams.

and, according to my native seer, we are just begun its trial.[22]

Before I slept, and part on her advice and part on a whim, I chewed one of the native woman's bulbs. As I placed it in my mouth, however, I was discovered out by Mackay and his minion, who asked for equal fare. Caught thus, and in the generally dire circumstances we all shared, I could not refuse them. The woman sleeps at my side each night, not out of fear of the men, who treat her with more respect than I have previously seen accorded a native woman, but from some curious authority in her which I do not question. We do not have carnal congress, but in her company my sleep is clean and unassailed by visions.

Since that sleep a full day has passed, or so they tell me. We struggled our way downstream until past noon, barely eluding boulder and embarra at least a dozen times. Then, as we were in midstream the river suddenly turned its course at an acute angle, and our two enemies came together with a vengeance. We paddled and poled the laden canoe as close to the bank as we could, but nearing it and likewise an enormous blockade of fallen trees, we took first a boulder across the canoe's bow, smashing it open, and then another to the rear that inflicted yet greater damage. Mackay leaped from the canoe in the instant I did in order to grapple for the shore, and Cancre bravely followed our example. But the water was too swift, and all three were swept from our footholds into the deeper water preceding the blockage. I recall swimming toward it, Mackay and Cancre in the front of me. I saw them disappear beneath it, and then I remember no more.[23]

Some number of hours have passed—it is dark. At least that I know for certain. My men tell that on our losing grip of the river bottom the canoe floundered and broke apart against the

---

[22]James Creek. In the mid-1970s, a group of interested local historians in B.C. attempted to have the name of James Creek changed back to Bad River. The argument used against them by the national archivist who handled the request in Ottawa was that Mackenzie himself did not actually name the creek, but rather referred only to its 'badness'. This journal rather conclusively backs the argument of those local historians.

[23]This is the point at which this journal begins to diverge significantly from the 1801 journal. In the absence of a concordance, which is outside the scope of the present project, I will refrain from commenting on the divergences.

huge embarra. The balance of its human cargo safely availed themselves of the sanctuary afforded by the embarra, taking along a small measure of the baggage. The rest followed beneath the waters. Panic and despair set in, as it seemed that the master and his principal aide were lost, and my men took to howls of grief. But the native woman fixed them with her authority and bade them to take heart, then made for the shore as if divinely instructed, and, crawling across the chaos of flooded debris to a spot preordained, is said to have intercepted me in the shallow water, drowned by all appearances, since my person was some quarter of an hour within the embarra before I emerged.

All my men declare themselves witnesses to this phenomenon, and I have no memory to argue against what surely is unexplainable and miraculous. I am me, and here I sit. This native saviour, urging my men by gesticulations, managed the reacquisition of the greater part of our essential baggage, save for the muskets and shot, and the majority of precious trade items. But there is no evidence of the fate of Mackay and Cancre, who seem utterly swept away. May whatever powers that control such things recover and relieve their souls.

The woman gathered together what items of my personal equipment she could, deposited them at my feet and bade me collect my thoughts by whatever means I knew, so that I might record my experience truly, digest its lesson, and determine the future of my crew and expedition. Thus saying, I fell into a vacant sulk that lasted an unknown time until I looked up to discover that my saviour had slipped away from me into the darkness, for reasons mysterious, and was quite gone from our company.

•

June 15, 1793

I am somewhat recovered today, except for the darkness covering my mind, the which I hide from the men with great effort. At the break of light, which now, approaching the solstice, is barely beyond its departure from the previous day, I arose in advance of my company, wrote down the yesterday events in my journal, then set to inventory the salvaged equipment. The canoe is altogether destroyed and gone, and save for two small fowling pieces, the musketry also. So too, our store of trade items is more reduced than at first calculated.

Our choice is to return by the route we have come or to forge ahead in the small hope of recovering our lost essentials, particularly the muskets. Neither alternative presages an easy survival, since the materials required for constructing a canoe are not readily available behind us, and the country to the fore is at best a blank to the men, if not to me. Yet only I am in possession of the information regarding the hostile natives said to be ahead, Mackay and Cancre having departed this world and taken their knowledges with them. Thankfully their recent separateness from the rest of the crew—which I have noted before with chagrin—has been severe enough that no member of the remainder is in posession of their confidences, the which at this point would be most damaging to my intentions. They are each and together in a funk, able only to bewail their fates without essential will as to their disposition.

None of these choices is attractive. If we were at the spot we stood at three days ago, I would give up my quest in a trice, following my under-instinct of that time. But here I see no way, in the present condition of the Bad River, that a return is possible. Thus we have but two choices. The first is to wait in this Hell of Hells until the river recedes from its flood enough to allow our return upstream. The second is to press on downstream in the hopes of acquiring some relief, be it from the massing insects or with the increase of opportunities to fish the waters, or finally, from the possible recovery, by chance, of some measure of our lost equipment.

Resolved within myself to venture downstream, I harangue the men, imbuing my argument for going forward with a warming dram of rum to each man, the casks of which have thankfully been recovered. One by one they fall in with my position, and by full morning light we are begun our agonizing advance out of this damnation, frequently wading through icy waters up to our waists or higher, and under the most cruel imaginable siege of insects.

But near midafternoon we are treated to yet another miracle, the which is, high on the side of an embarra, the remnant of our canoe. How it proceeded through the intervening miles, having aleady disappeared beneath a jam in plain sight and having since then passed across several similar blockades, I do not know. But the craft is repairable within our present capabilities, and its use will greatly ease our passage. The men are astonished, and reward my faithfulness to our grand pursuit with a mixture of awe and enthusiasm for my foresight, to which I respond with a dram of rum and exhortations toward the swift repair of the craft. This repair is speedily carried out, and in the highest of spirits. And as we worked to the repair, our remaining native,[24] forging somewhat downstream to scout the river, fell full upon a deer, which he was able to approach and take with no more for a weapon than the spearpoint notched upon the crown of his bow. Thus we are supplied with fresh meat. Soon we are again on the river with our reduced load of men and baggage. The river seems less aggressive here, but that may be a misperception directed by our improved spirits.

•

June 16, 1793

This day's events strain the credibility of those previous to it, which of themselves are of unparalleled strangeness. After the recovery and repair of our canoe, the river seemed to lessen in its rages, enabling us for the most part to remain on its currents, although, with the warming of the weather, the predations by the insects grew more savage. By midmorning we were out of the Bad River into a much wider stream that in its turn soon fell in with another, yet larger stream.[25] The canoe, however, having barely withstood its latest punishments, and with the poor materials which we have used to repair it, was in such a state of collapse that we were required to hover near the bank for fear

---

[24]It is unclear who this man is. He is never named, or otherwise mentioned in any context that allows his tribe to be established.

[25]The first stream is Herrick Creek. The second is the McGregor River, which runs into the Fraser River.

that it might break apart wholly and sink our remaining supplies.

Despite this, the men were in a state of considerable cheerfulness, convinced that, temporarily at least, the worst was over, and having forgotten, being of shallow memory, that we are defenseless against either hostile natives or the need to hunt bigger game. I myself await with some anxiety the place prophesied in the many dreams, although my fears were calmed at our entrance into the second large river, which seemed to bear westward by a southerly leaning. I busied myself with compass and sextant readings, then took a small measure of blissful slumber.

I was awakened by the rough shaking of my person by one of my men, and the news that fires were visible ahead. The fires, however, were a goodly distance away, and I attempted to calm the general anxiety they produced, the which was fueled by their belated remarking of our relative defenselessness. I gave a short lecture to them concerning the great importance of maintaining a calm exterior when the time came, as it almost certainly would, to face such peoples as controlled the regions along the river. That we should posture a general superiority and fearlessness, I told them, was our best defence, hiding from them my private estimation of our vulnerability.

Their anxieties were somewhat relieved by a sudden abundance of deer along the northwesterly river banks, in numbers the like of which we have not seen since entering these mountainous regions. At one promontory, where we stopped to effect a patching of our decrepit boat, the deer were wholly tamed, walking directly toward us so that one of the men was able to take hold on the animal of his choice and crudely break its neck.

Also novel to my eye was a species of tall egrets of a bizarre pinkish hue, with misshapen bills and extreme elongated legs. As we passed, these birds stood quite still in their places, as if frozen.[26]

About this time there appeared on the northerly bank of the river a subtle mist, which, as we let the current carry us, deepened

---

[26]The species of this bird is unknown, and they are not mentioned in the 1801 journal. One can only speculate: glossy ibises, spoonbills, or a now-extinct variety of flamingo.

considerably until it could be penetrated by the eye no more than a few yards in advance. Given the fragility of our craft I decided not to cross the stream, where the mists seemed thinner, and took the opposite tack, moving even closer to the banks, where, should an accident accost us, a passage onto shore was sure. This was of itself an extreme piece of good fortune, for had our canoe been sound we would have missed the spot. As it was, the mists suddenly ended, and we found ourselves on the verge of a nearly completed oxbow, which presently stood as a barely currented backwater surrounding an island. On the outer banks of the island milled veritable herds of deer.

And on that island, defying logic, stood a fine stone cottage almost identical to the one in which I spent several weeks in Sussex in the company of the woman of my recent dreams. Yet this cottage possessed several remarkable additions: a substantially built storehouse similar to that at Ft. Chipewyan, and, sitting upon the cottage's stone steps, my lately disappeared assistant, Mackay, and his cohort Cancre!

A great whooping and shouting was instantly taken up by both sides, and the great joy with which my crew gave forth caused the canoe to flounder and break up on the spot, the men so eager to embrace their lost comrades that I had to exercise great restraint upon them to prevent further damage or loss to our baggage. Upon gaining the shore, however, I hung back, having sighted a third person, familiar only to myself, standing behind my two renewed companions within the shelter of the porch.

In my turn I embraced both men, and expressed my joy and wonderment at their fortuitous condition. Then I took Mackay aside to question him. I quickly found him to be in a state of considerable mental confusion. Like myself, he recalled little after being swept beneath the embarra. But for him the period of blankness was not a few minutes, but more than a day. Nor did it seem that the Cancre had been his saviour, for that worthy alike had known nothing for the same dark interval. Mackay said that he had wakened on a soft bed inside the stone cottage, the Cancre beside him on an adjoining cot, still deep in slumber.

Mackay avowed that he had felt his body to be quite refreshed, as if awakening from a leisurely sleep. Yet looking down upon his limbs, he had discovered them somewhat bloated, the skin cobbled as if soaked in water, and although these effects were forgotten in the awakening of his companion, an unease captured him that still persisted. As he spoke about these matters he seemed somewhat vague in his steps as if his body were unwilling to heed his will, and I had to hold him up to prevent his tottering. Also were his eyes curiously milky in hue, as if coated by some foreign substance. I sat him down and bade him rest, and found the Cancre, who was standing amongst the men at their urging, but with the same uncertain posture I had noted in Mackay and the same subtle milkiness of eye. For a moment their aimlessness resembled that of the deer that abounded on the premises, but I put that thought from my mind.

I set the men to securing the baggage from the shore, which included the butchering of the recently captured deer, and to laying out the soaked equipment to dry in the sun. Then I entered the house. It was indeed she who greeted me from within, and she bade me enter and sit by her. And yet it was not she. Her garb was simpler than I recalled, her composure deeply formal. She wore a simple white smock, buttoned at regular intervals up the front. The cloth was fine linen, and at her side, in a narrow belt, was a set of heavy keys. Her blond hair was cut simply, and was tied by a single thong to reveal her countenance unencumbered.

My heart locked with terror, but notwithstanding my fears, I was fair bursting with questions. She seemed willing to await my speech, and it was not long before my questions won out over my fear. They spewed out in a torrent, and my eagerness brought laughter from her.

"If you will be patient, my dear Mr. Alexander Mackenzie," said she, "I will answer your questions as far as I am worthy. But first, let me assure you as to the health of your two men and to the safety of all your equipment which the savage river removed. These items now rest in my storeroom, along with additional supplies for the renovation of your canoe."

Then our conversation traversed my questions, yet I detected a certain obtuseness in her method of answer such that the substance of my need for fact was not satisfied, but rather, shaped into an always narrowing field of debate marked by a subtle but growing generality and opaqueness. After an hour or two of this I could relate to myself less information than I began my questions in possession of, such that I can relate here no understanding of the passage and purpose of the woman to this place, nor the information and logic leading to an understanding of the saving of the lives of Mackay and Cancre. Instead, I feel the strengthening of my former ambition and resolve, and a sense of the irrelevance of the present despite its mysteries.

At length I departed from her company, having learned next to nothing from her, and retreated to this journal to record what little I can.

•

June 18,1793

I write this passage in the canoe some few miles downstream from the island, which we departed this afternoon. It will be, I fear, my last entry of this variety, since I cannot avoid a growing conviction that pursuing it is a waste of time, and that I were better to record, as I have in the other book, the simple notations of time and landscape, and matters of easily established fact.

Let me therefore establish the few facts I have acquired, after which I will indulge myself to some last speculations concerning their meaning. First, I do not know the purpose of the island, nor how it came to be built upon this wilderness I thought myself the first man of European origins to invade. Second, Mackay and Cancre are indeed alive and well, although somewhat altered. Both men seem greatly subdued, as if their experience between the dangerous embarra that removed them from our company and our recovery of their persons at the island has removed the persuasions of mind that have, through the course of this voyage, separated them from myself and the balance of our fellowship. Mackay seems utterly uninterested in his previous botanic pursuits, such that when I exposed my supply of bulbs to him, he showed neither recognition nor interest. Instead, he busies himself with the renovation of the canoe, and with speculations as to the advancing of the fur trade likely along this route. Cancre likewise

39

busies himself with preparations for hunting and fishing with simplicity and the concentration borne of it. As a test of this I have questioned him concerning the readings of Mr. Shakespeare he has received from Mackay, and his memorization of what he has heard, and he admitted no knowledge of either. Mackay still possesses the volume, but when I entreated him to show it to the bemused Cancre he seemed unaware that he had such an item, and subsequently abandoned it on the steps of the cottage.

The woman employed as the proprietor of the cottage is indeed the woman I knew in England. I have spent the greater part of the last two days in her company. She seems much changed in some ways. Her mind contains great subtleties, the which I could not penetrate but was rather penetrated by. My recall of our conversations is extremely weak and seems to fade further with each of my attempts to bring them back.

As I lay in the comfort of her boudoir, the familiar likeness of which was so unexpected in this wildness, I heard cries of the nightbirds identical to those I heard so vividly during my sojourn in England. But where they brought me great tranquility then, here they struck a sourer note, like gibberish, settling me not to sweet repose but to fearful nightmares, in which I was lodged among the dead and dying in a great stone mausoleum lined wall by wall with the goods essential to profitable trade with the natives: the long strings of worthless beads and buttons, and the packets of mirrors and cheap implements by which the natives are easily convinced to part with their heretofore dearest possessions.

With these and similar visions I felt a deep depression falling over me, one so great that I departed her comforts and walked outdoors to sleep on the cold ground in the company of my men, who slept so deeply they were as if dead, the deer able to mingle amongst them at their ease, and here and there lying down to sleep among them with such familiarity that the bodies of deer and men were draped across the other in bizarre embraces.

Before I slept, I chewed one of the bulbs given me by the departed native woman, thinking it might provide me with a easier sleep. Yet when I slept again the white woman again pursued me into my dreams, offering first the ecstasy of lust, the which I refused, and then the pretence of explaining herself and this place,

40

which even in the throes of nightmare I continued to crave understanding of. One speech from this I recall clearly. It is perhaps a gift derived from the eating of the bulb, and although the contents are surely the purest phantasmagoria, I will record it here.

"This is the power and the outcome," said she, turning to her storehouse of trinkets and beads with a grandiose sweep of her arms. "From it will come mastery over the unnumbered heathens. The ecstasies you took of my body, the fermenting of liberty in the minds of common men, the puny wisdoms of this wilderness provided you by the native woman, all are phantasms from which no gain can be had. Only in ambition is the certainty of mind from which true power grows. For you, that is what this place is. And your powers will grow from here, until the distractions of the animated world will become opaque and lost to you and to your men, and to your recording of its commotion. By its loss will mastery be gained.[27]

"In time you will forget this place, and all you have seen here. Even I will be forgotten. Right now your memory fades, and in a month, a year, little more, all will be gone. Then you will turn in wholeness to your quest, where your vision will prevail, your ambitions be gratified. You will have children, wealth, the company and admiration of the high-born. And until those things come to pass you will be impervious to further mortal dangers, although not to the setbacks of fortune. And in these lands, what you have begun will be carried to completion.

"And what will you give up? You will have women, and you will be their master, as men were meant to be. You will have power over men weaker than you, and men who are above you will seek your company out of fear of your ambition. The liberty that attracted you will expose itself as illusion soon enough. The poor shall stay poor, the rich will heap riches upon riches. You will

---

[27]There is an indication that the physical trauma of Mackenzie's near drowning has produced a series of visual and intellectual hallucinations. Despite the coherence of this philosophical tract, one can assume an altered state of consciousness that proved temporary, since Mackenzie ceased to write in this journal, and the 1801 Journal factually repudiates the alleged drowning and the existence of the island and the two women, native and European.

lose nothing, Alexander Mackenzie, you will give up nothing. There is nothing to contemplate in this wilderness, and much to be gained, much to be transformed by ambition and force."

I slept well into the midmorning, and even then had to forcibly waken my men, who gave every intention of wanting to sleep until doomsday. To a man, after waking, they evinced a strong desire to depart, for reasons I'm sure they had no notion of. I felt their urge doubly; I wanted to escape with the small fund of my understanding and memory that remains, and secondly to save my tattered sanity. As the distance between our canoe and the island grows, my sanity returns, but in measure to its return, my understanding of what I have seen grows dull.

I know not what to do from here except to continue along the river. Thus, after I finish the recording of this passage, I will wrap the journal in its deerskin and push it to the bottom of my luggage, where I may one day examine its contents at my leisure. But now I must shake off the bottoming accidie, and settle accounts with the dying light to the westward.

The Endako Hotel Massacre

Most people in the north heard about the Endako Hotel Massacre. As the years passed the Massacre's fame reached even further—and why not? All in all, it's an interesting story. Or maybe I should say "stories", because there's more than one story involved.

When stories spread, they don't travel intact from one person to another. That's more or less obvious. The truth gets stretched. The facts become distorted—or the facts are forgotten. But what also happens with some stories as they drift away from precise fact is that what is lost of the factual truth is picked up in an archetypal truth; the story starts to talk about those intangible truths that pertain to everyone and everything. When that happens, you have myth: a story that operates accurately both within and outside the everyday world, and connects you to the deepest passions and intelligences of the human species. You not only experience such a story as personal entertainment, you learn from it. It takes you into a larger dimension of reality. A world. It is not so much a fiction as it is an inheritance.

I'm not sure whether it's because this story takes place in the north or because it takes place in the "modern" world that some peculiar things occurred as it was told and retold. First, the factual events, and the motivations that caused them to occur, were covered up right from the beginning. The wandering archetypes that are said to inhabit the collective imagination of human beings have therefore attached themselves, in this story, to the coverup. To a lie.

The easy way to deal with it would be to believe that the story, in its currently accepted version, will talk about those intangible *lies* that pertain to everyone and everything, thus putting it in the realm of truth anyway. We would have, by this process, anti-myths and anti-archetypes. That would be nice and symmetrical, and it would neatly reflect, in a cynical sort of way, the history of the modern world, which if you think about it, is really pretty much a record of coverups and public lies, and the narratives that attach themselves to those.

But that isn't quite what happens with the Endako Hotel Massacre. And this is where it takes on a slightly sinister cast. As it turns out, the reasons why the facts were covered up reveal some typical truths about the way people live their private lives in the north (and everywhere else in this civilization, as far as I can see). All that those seemingly small and unassailable truths tell us is why there is nothing to this civilization now but a collection of isolated private lives.

•

Here is the currently accepted version of the Endako Hotel Massacre:

In the winter of 1942, during the period when Allied war fortunes seemed darkest, three men checked into a small hotel at Endako, a railroad weigh station some 150 gravel miles west of Prince George by road, and, as the crow flies, about 300 miles from the Pacific Ocean. All three men wore snap-brim hats, suits, and wool overcoats, and they appeared young and able-bodied enough to cause one to wonder about why they weren't in the armed forces fighting Fascism. They arrived in two relatively new automobiles, two men in one, the third in the other. They checked into the hotel quietly, rented separate rooms, and carried their small kitbags up to these rooms. About an hour later, they came downstairs together, entered the small cafe in the hotel, and ate dinner. Throughout dinner, according to the elderly Chinese man who ran the cafe, they spoke quietly but with some animation, stopping only when he came to bring tea or to collect empty dishes. They finished their dinners, complimented him on the meal, and returned to their rooms.

About an hour before midnight, the two other guests who were staying in the hotel began to hear disturbing noises from the rooms the men occupied: crashing sounds and loud voices. For a time, the noise spilled out into the hallway, but the other guests, prudent men, stayed inside their rooms. The noise abruptly ceased after several shots were heard.

The next morning, the owner of the hotel, who had slept through it all, discovered that all three rooms were a shambles. Most of the furniture in them had been destroyed, including the beds. A bicycle one of the other guests had left in the hall was found in one of the destroyed rooms, along with a number of the water buckets that in those days served as fire extinguishers. There had been an attempt to wash sections of the floor, and the owner found evidence that blood had been spilled in at least one of the rooms. The men, all three of them, had vanished in their cars.

Two days later, an army truck arrived and a squad of closed-mouthed soldiers combed the surrounding woods for several days. They bivouacked in the railroad depot, and neither socialized with nor even deigned to speak to the locals.

For the next few weeks, the people of Endako thought and talked about little other than this odd and relatively thrilling sequence of events. Within a month, the facts were settled in their minds: the three men were agents, and had had some sort of falling out during the evening they spent in the hotel. One or more of them had been shot, and the remaining agent or agents had disposed of the body or bodies nearby. The generally agreed upon theory was that at least one of the agents was from an enemy power, probably Germany, since all three agents were fair-complected Caucasians.

It was agreed that the soldiers who appeared shortly afterward

45

must have been looking for buried bodies, the escaped agents, or the secret documents the agents were trading (the Chinese man had recalled that they were passing documents of some sort back and forth after dinner). Speculation on what the soldiers found varied according to which of the locals was doing the speculating. Some said they found a body or bodies, and others said they found nothing. Someone suggested that perhaps the troops themselves were enemy soldiers, there to look for the documents, thus accounting for the fact that they had not spoken to the locals—they were afraid their foreign accents would give away their identities.

One man insisted that they were actually Italian soldiers, an observation based on their dark hair and dark eyes. He further theorized that they had nothing to do with the agents in the hotel, but rather were an advance party for the then much-feared Japanese invasion. The woods, the man said, were now laid with mines. This theory gained a great deal of credibility some weeks later when a train derailed, although it was argued by others that the cause of the derailment was a careless piece of track-switching by one of the local railroad employees. Even so, people began to stay clear of that section of the woods.

As time went on the differences of opinion concerning the identities of the men and the events themselves became more varied. For more than a year almost every fight that went on in the hotel bar was a direct result of an argument over the "true facts" of the Massacre, as it was now commonly called.

The months turned into years, with the Massacre as the constant topic of local speculation and talk. It was Endako's little piece of the war, and the citizens of Endako held onto it passionately, more so as the threat of a Japanese invasion began to fade and the village became, in the minds of the locals, less of a potential front-line of the war and more of what it had always been—a little bit of nowhere. The controversy reignited into full flame for a while in the fall of 1944, when Allied Intelligence, having gleaned a few rumours about the story, sent a stiffly formal young British captain to investigate. He listened to all the different versions and left again without giving the locals the slightest hint of his own opinion on the matter.

46

•

I first learned of the Endako Hotel Massacre about ten years after the war ended. I was a schoolboy, and by that time the story of the Massacre was the stuff that schoolboys dream of. Certain parts of the story had petrified by then, while others, with the elasticity of legend, had continued to grow. Two of the formally dressed men were now unquestionably German agents. The third man was a Canadian counter-espionage agent sent to uncover the Axis plan for the invasion of the west coast of North America. At some point during that fateful first evening, the German agents must have discovered his identity, and fearful of their fate at the hands of a disappointed German High Command, attempted to murder him. They succeeded only in wounding the brave and resourceful Canadian, and he was able to escape into the night on foot with the invasion plans. The German agents then ditched his car (an automobile was found in the Challako River during low water in 1947), and began to hunt him. But despite his wounds, the Canadian eluded them by using his superior skills as a woodsman. Informed of this dangerous situation by their embarrassed but loyal agents, the German High Command quickly sent in a regiment of disguised Italian commandos. They had no more luck in flushing out their quarry than had the agents.

The Canadian, after considerable tribulation, escaped from the commandos by building a makeshift canoe from birchbark and spruce gum, and reached the safety of civilization. Several crack Canadian commando units were swiftly dispatched, and they lured the Italians from their bivouac near Endako, then ambushed them deep in the woods some thirty miles to the north. They took no prisoners, not wanting to alarm the locals or alert the Axis that their invasion plans were now in Allied hands. One Italian commando, however, did escape, and after switching some tracks that caused a series of troop-train derailments, made his way back to a rendezvous point.

Due to the Italian commando's report of Allied preparedness, the planned invasion of North America was thereby postponed and, as we all know, never took place.

Somewhere out in the bush north of Endako are the unmarked

47

graves of more than 200 Italian soldiers along with an untold number of live mines. No one has ever gone out looking for the gravesites because of the mines.

Around the time I first heard the story, I asked my uncle, a commercial traveller who'd often passed through Endako, what he knew about the Massacre.

"Well," he said, "I've heard something about it. But first, why don't you tell me what you've heard?"

He listened to my story carefully, and when I finished, he laughed very strangely.

"Have I got it about right?" I asked.

"I think you're a bit off the mark in a few of the details," he said, still chuckling to himself, "but you've certainly made it into a wonderful story."

Beyond that, though, he wouldn't talk about it. No matter how I pestered him, he just grinned and told me that I had 'a great story'.

•

As I grew older, I lost interest in the Massacre. To my adolescent mind, it was ancient history, and I had other, more immediate fish to fry. But every few years the Massacre would surface again, and I noticed that each time I heard the story it was more spectacular: invariably there were more troops and equipment involved, and more bloodshed. The Italian regiment became a Japanese division replete with tanks and Zeros, and all were buried in the Endako forests, surrounded by landmines. What alone seemed to remain constant in the tale was the part about the three men and the wrecking of the Endako Hotel. They came in two cars, ate dinner in the hotel cafe, exchanged documents and retired to their rooms. Then they fought their part of the battle, destroyed everything in their rooms, and were gone the next morning, having made an attempt to disguise the fact that there had been blood-letting.

•

About four years ago I visited my uncle. He'd long since retired, and had settled happily into his leisure. He was by now getting on in years, but his eyes remained alert and clear, and a wreath of inviting laugh wrinkles indicated that even if the end of his life was closing in on him, he was satisfied with what he knew and what he'd done in the world.

For several hours we sat on his front porch drinking iced tea and watching the northern summer deepen into yet another gorgeous autumn. We talked in general terms about how kindly the powers that be had treated him, and how pleased he was to have received their blessings. Then, to my surprise, he brought up the subject of the Massacre.

"Incidentally, how's the story going?" he asked, as if our conversation of years ago had taken place yesterday.

"How's what story going?"

"Your story about the Massacre up at Endako. You recall the one."

I told him the last version I'd heard, with all the intervening embellishments. By the time I was finished, he was laughing so hard I feared for his health. But he soon gained control over his mirth, and settled back in his chair.

"Do you want to know what really happened?" he asked, breaking into a renewed chuckle.

"I thought you told me you didn't know anything about it," I replied, puzzled.

"Oh, I knew, all right," he said. "I just didn't think it would be much of a story for a kid. The one you had back then suited you just fine."

"Tell me the real story."

"Think you're old enough to handle it?" he asked.

I said I was, and watched as he sucked in his lower lip, trying to decide on the best way to begin.

"I was a traveller in those days, you know," he began. "And with the War being on everything was rationed. The things we had to sell our customers were rationed like everything else, and so was gasoline. You can imagine what kind of spot that put us in. We didn't so much sell our products as distribute them among the customers we liked best, just like a bunch of little Hitlers.

Even then there was never enough to go around. Our biggest problem was gasoline—we never had enough. So, to save on gas, and because there was nothing really to compete over, a lot of us travellers rode together. We didn't tell the head office we were doing it, because not telling them allowed us to put in separate expense sheets.

"Actually, we had a hell of a good time in those years. There wasn't any point in hustling, so we spent most our free time fooling around, playing practical jokes on one another. Some weeks we didn't go out at all. We just phoned our customers and told them what they were getting, and they just said, well, thank you, Sir, I appreciate it. That summer—1942, as a matter of fact, I built most of this house while I was supposed to be out on my territory.

"Bum McKillop—you may remember him—and I were best friends in those days. He was the salesman for my competition, but we rode together most of the time for nearly two years. This one trip we made out west together, we happened to run across another salesman in Burns Lake. Harvey something—I can't recall his last name, but he was a happy-go-lucky sort, and I suppose he's passed on by now."

My uncle's features darkened for a moment, and he fell silent. I let him drift, and after a moment he looked up and seemed almost surprised to see me there.

"Oh. Well. We decided to drive to Endako that evening, and stay in the same hotel together. We checked in—the owner knew us and was always glad to see us—had our dinner, and went upstairs to retire for the evening.

"We played some cards in Bum's room for a while, then turned in. About 10:30 p.m., I heard a knock on my door, and Bum yelling at me to open up. I was nearly asleep, but he made it sound urgent enough that I stumbled over to the door and turned the knob. The door opened, and it was Bum all right—with a bucket of water.

"Well, the war was on, as they say. I chased him all around the hotel, and when I couldn't catch him, I decided that the best thing I could do was dismantle his bed so he wouldn't get any sleep either. And while I was doing that he went into my room and took *my* bed apart. We woke Harvey up, but when he came out and saw what we were doing he went back into his room and locked the door on us. But of course we'd made such a mess in our rooms that we decided we couldn't let him go scot-free. So we filled up buckets of water and knocked on his door.

"We called for him to come out, but he wasn't having any of that. Then Bum noticed that the transom window over his door was open. So we talked him into coming to the door so we could whisper a secret to him, and he fell for it. Just as he was telling us we wouldn't get him, we lofted both buckets through the transom and soaked him.

"Well, he let out a roar and started chasing us. I went one way, and Bum the other, and when he took off after Bum I went into his room and did the job on everything in there. About the time I was finished, Bum rode in on a bicycle someone had left in the hall, lost his balance and nearly went on out through the window. I grabbed him just as he was about go through, and broke the window myself trying to hold him in. Cut my arm quite seriously, see?"

He rolled back his sleeve and showed me a deep scar about two inches long.

"That put an end to the fun," he continued. "We had to go downstairs and wake up the owner so I could get bandaged up. He wasn't too pleased when he found out what we'd been up to, as you can imagine. But we paid him for the broken window, cleaned up a little, and gave him an extra ten dollars. The next morning we checked out early and went on our separate ways."

"Then what happened?" I asked. "How did the story come about that you were espionage agents?"

"I'm not exactly sure. Part of it, I guess, was that the owner of the hotel decided to have a little fun, and I think he also decided that this was an opportunity to collect some money out of the government for the damages we'd caused. So he and the Chinaman from the cafe cooked up a cock-and-bull story about some enemy agents wrecking the place. It worked fine. He got a few customers he wouldn't have had otherwise, and I believe he even got some new furniture out of the deal."

"Why didn't you say something about it?"

"I couldn't. None of us could. First of all, the owner of the hotel was one of our customers. It's not a good idea to tell tales on your customers. And if we had, our head offices would have found out we were travelling together, and that would have meant big trouble. And I guess we didn't want to confess to having torn apart a hotel like a bunch of ten-year-old boys. We were supposed to be salesmen, representing important firms in a serious way. And after a while the story got so big that I don't think anyone would have believed us even if we'd tried to tell them the truth.''

"What about the Italian commandos?''

"There was a squad of soldiers around, but they were there to check the tracks for sabotage. The Army did that regularly, up and down the entire line. The only peculiarity was that this particular squad was French-Canadian. They didn't talk to the locals because they couldn't speak English.''

"Does anyone else know the truth?'' I asked.

"Well,'' he chuckled, "*We* all did, and now you do. And I suppose the owner had to tell that Army Intelligence officer at least part of the truth. The Army must have decided that since no one got hurt, it was good propaganda. Everything's gone now, even the hotel. It was torn down when the big mining companies came in.''

My uncle got up from his chair and stretched his frail body. Then he looked at me gravely.

"I don't much care what you do with all this,'' he said. "For me, it's just about all up anyway. But try to remember, whatever you do, that you have to respect the truth as it finds you.''

•

So that's the truth of the Massacre—not a heroic war story at all, just some salesmen having a good time and getting ahead in life. Nothing so terrible in that, is there? At first, I agreed, accepting my uncle's facts about the Massacre as a charming bringdown to a wildly inflated tale. But then I began to wonder why the story had become so inflated, and why it had nothing to do with the actuality of my uncle's life and those of the other two commercial travellers.

52

In a civilization where the truth, as David Hume discovered more than two centuries ago, is no more than a species of sensation, factual accounts are going to tell us "the real story" whether we like it or not. And a "real" story is always about how people imagine the world they inhabit, and how they want to live in it. The factual whats, whys, wheres, and whens are of secondary importance.

My problem with my uncle and his "facts" is that all the essentials remain utterly hidden. First, the only thing that got massacred in Endako was the truth, and along with it, the kind of world in which people are able to hold onto a sense that reality has more dimension and depth than the single focus of their personal well-being. Second, this kindly man was a detached spectator in life. In a more difficult world, his detachment would have made him the victim of every circumstance, and he probably wouldn't have ended up kindly, or for that matter, old. It is only that he lived in a period of wealth and environmental surplus that allowed him to ignore the planet and the human society around him.

I'm not arguing about what kind of man my uncle was and still is. He's been a decent, hardworking man all his life. I'm very fond of him, and I respect his down-to-earth sense of himself. But I understood what he meant when he reversed the old maxim about respecting the truth as you find it. He was saying what he'd always said, and what he'd practised: he hadn't made the world, he'd just lived in it as best he could, taking advantage of whatever opportunities presented themselves.

I'm not my uncle, and his story sticks in my craw, even though I grew up with the same basic values and attitudes he has. He didn't have to see the big picture or the whole story. I have to at least try to. I'm a writer, and however ridiculous it may seem, it's my job to imagine a world—a whole one—every time I write a story.

I guess that makes me see the "facts" a little differently. Sure, the towns all grew bigger, and industry after new industry came in to provide jobs and develop the countryside. Some people got wealthy, and some people got killed. Most of them got to live out their lives the way my uncle has: with a fair degree of kindness and concern for others, and with a reasonable degree of comfort. But now the best forests have been used up, the mills and the mines are closing down one after another, the rivers are fouled—everyone who reads this knows what I'm talking about, so I won't flog it any further. The surplus is gone.

So what is it that I'm fussing about, anyway? Well, I'm fussing because I think we're all endangered by the coverups, and by the phoney legends that get built on them. They're about to collapse under us. Lies always do that. And this isn't science fiction. I can't say that there isn't such a thing in the universe as anti-matter, but I can say categorically that anti-myths and anti-archetypes are not meaningful terms. Myth and archetype are fancy names for the connective tissue that binds the individual to the species and to the planet. They are perfectly, solely, social. And their contraries do not, by some bizarre physics, add up to the same thing. They add up to what we have.

There's no world possible with these lies. Inferred or implied, they produce no coherent view of the human community and those parts of the planet that now depend on the technology and good will of human society for their maintenance: no shareable archetypes, no myth.

Lies merely reproduce *themselves*. The shallow ethics of private self-interest with its rhetoric hides an assumption. The assumption is that because self-interest has served the individual quite well in this brief frontier world of artificial surplus, self-interest is enlightened and benevolent, that it is enough. *And that is a lie.*

As the writer of this story, seeing the frontier collapse in ruin, the surpluses dwindle, and hearing the lies become more transparent each day, the rhetoric more shrill, I have to raise the only question that really matters: what will our children inherit, and what kinds of stories will be told to them?

Icarus

Icarus was the son of Daedalus, the famed technologist of Athens. Unlike his father, who was a master builder of a great many wondrous things, only imprudence marks the short life of Icarus. His father was one of those truly remarkable men the genetic pool occasionally provides for the species, as multi-faceted as he was inventive, and both of those characteristics were energized by an independence of mind and a lust for adventure. Hence, in the political wilderness of early Mediterranean civilization, man and boy travelled widely, most often as guests of ambitious princes, but more than once as prisoners. It is during one of these periods of captivity, on the island of Crete, that we become interested in Icarus.

For some long-forgotten moral recalcitrance on the part of Daedalus, or perhaps because of some technical problem he could not quickly solve, father and son were imprisoned in the Labyrinth of Minos, a structure which Daedalus himself had earlier built for the Cretan king in order to house the latest in a long line of intermodal monsters. To escape from it, the great technologist constructed the first flying machines, made of feathers, wood and wax. He somehow tested them (although this is hard to imagine if we recall that the Labyrinth was, according to legend, a cave) and deemed them workable. Then, standing atop a high precipice that overlooked the sea (still, we must assume, within the Labyrinth) he tied one of the contraptions to his son and gave him some advice about how to fly it: don't fly too low or too high, and don't try to navigate by yourself.

"Follow me," he said sternly to Icarus. "Don't try to think on your own. My path is the only one, so follow it exactly."

Icarus thought his father was only moralizing at him, which, like most powerful and preoccupied fathers, Daedalus indulged in all too frequently. 'Business is business,' 'Don't go off by yourself,' and 'Stay away from the minotaur' were familiar cautionary homilies to the young man, and this latest advice seemed little different. It meant nothing to him, since to this point in his short life nothing of his father's complex reality had touched him. But unbeknownst to Daedalus, while he had been constructing the flying machines, Icarus had conceived a contraption of his own: he had determined that he could and should fly by his will alone.

•

The human impulse to fly originates far back in the opaque past, long before the Labyrinth was built, and long before will and technology began to interact, and to fill our world with wreckage. Perhaps one afternoon, at leisure, someone pointed out to his or her companions a flight of migrating birds. No doubt there were replies—grunts of incomprehension and indifference. But among the company someone sighed, and in this fusion of curiosity, wonder and will, the fate of Icarus—the perfect instance of the impulse to fly—was sealed.

Daedalus knew nothing of what was going on in the mind of his heretofore docile son. He was, as always, preoccupied with tangible problems. And sure that he'd established adequate flight safety regulations in the mind of the child, he launched himself from the cliff. After a significant and insolent pause, Icarus followed. Out over the cliffs they drifted, away (the story goes) from the imprisoning Labyrinth. At first they probably seemed like drunken vultures, but as each in his own way gained control over his contraption, they began to fly with a subtle and unmistakably human grace.

All this took place to the puzzlement of some peasants who were collecting shellfish at the base of the precipice, and who instantly began to argue amongst themselves over whether the flyers were gods or very large buzzards. Later on, the more patient observers recognized that the flyers were actually men with contraptions, and they rushed home to tell their friends this remarkable news. Initially, their friends were not impressed.

"Gods, kings, and men," they snorted, "are always leaping from high places in ridiculous contraptions. Why should we think this believable or interesting? Since you obviously found nothing valuable in the wreckage, what's the use of it?"

Only then did their informants tell them that the contraptions were successful ones, that they had not crashed, and that the men operating them were now far out at sea.

Meanwhile, Daedalus and Icarus flew without incident toward the mainland of Greece. They travelled quite a long distance before the inevitable occurred. Icarus' small fund of caution was overtaken by his will, and he began to indulge in some aerial acrobatics. The rushing air stripped the wax from the feathers on his contraption, and he spun out of control, crashed into the sea and quickly sank beneath Homer's winedark waves.

End of Icarus, sort of. Except that miles away back in the village, the peasants now *believed* in the flight of Icarus and Daedalus. Having easily discovered the flyers' identities at the palace gates, they were already concocting wild exaggerations about the flight, the character and personal histories of the flyers, and what this might soon mean for inter-island travel.

Serious students of aeronautics, incidentally, will insist that the Icarus story is purely symbolic, or that it is the record of an elaborate ancient hoax. They will tell you that no construct such as the one devised by Daedalus could glide much further than the distance from the top of the precipice to the clam beach beneath it. And to be sure, there is even a modest rumour amongst the more obscure ancient storytellers that Daedalus escaped the Labyrinth by boat, and that Icarus drowned when he tripped and fell overboard during the night voyage.

Well, you can argue this out with those peasants who witnessed the launch if you're certain that no one actually flew. Or with the peasants who, a few days later, found and buried the battered contraption of wax, wood, and feathers that washed up on the beach.

If you do argue it with them, it will be to no avail. You will get no satisfaction because you'll have asked the only questions that don't matter to them. And quite frankly, I agree with their stance. Who cares if Daedalus and Icarus *really* flew? What matters is whether the flight was fated one way or another, whether they managed to escape from the Labyrinth, and what is to be learned from the wreckage.

•

The story of the Lockheed P-38 Lightning, statistically at least, is much more certain. For one thing, it clearly did fly, although it looked as improbable in the air as Daedalus and Icarus must have. It was a twin-engined, twin-fuselage aircraft with a fifty-two foot wingspan and a thirty-seven foot overall length. It cruised at 290 miles per hour and could reach a maximum speed of 414 miles per hour. Between 1937 and 1945, more than 5000 of them were built. Its distinct silhouette, its firepower and its unusual maneuverability made its German victims call it *Der Gabelschwantz Tuefel*—the fork-tailed devil—but those who flew the P-38 said it was a difficult plane, with a tendency to crash for no apparent reason. Still, it was much admired by children and by adults of vivid imagination: Antoine de St. Exupery, for example, loved the aircraft, and when he died late in 1944, it was because he crashed his P-38 into a Normandy hillside.

After 1943 the P-38 began to be replaced by the more conventional Lockheed P-51 Mustang, a smaller, more reliable aircraft that stirred less excitement in those who watched it from the ground. That's how I get into this story.

When I was a child growing up in northern British Columbia,

58

the P-38 stirred the deepest part of my imagination. The slightest mention of one could send me off into hours of daydreams in which I was the pilot of my own P-38. This aircraft, which I'd had specially equipped, was capable of taking on and defeating not only the already long-vanquished Germans and Japanese, but the combined forces of communism, parents and teachers. On the wall of my bedroom above my bed hung a framed photograph of one, and every time I looked at that photograph I cursed the silent gods that I was too young to have flown a real P-38 in real combat.

It has been my fate to be born at the beginning of the uneasy peace that holds today, a peace in which wars are fought without being declared; the peace which forfends the very ideas of fate and utopia, replacing them with the ancient and circular notions of labyrinth and inescapable doom. Maybe my love for P-38s was my way of saying to hell with the future and with that doom.

You will therefore not be too surprised to know that when a real P-38 touched down at the local airport one spring afternoon in 1956, I knew that it was an omen. Its presence in my world was a miracle, and I just happened to be in need of a miracle. I was a twelve-year-old baseball player, a second-string shortstop trying to make the team of Little League All-Stars that was soon to represent our town at the district championship tournament. Hardly heroic in scale, those ambitions, but I was not a child of heroic stature. I was like Icarus must have been: self-occupied, and secretly, irrelevantly willful.

The aircraft, likewise, was not there for heroic deeds. According to the local radio and newspaper, it was there to take aerial photographs of the vast tracts of virgin forest that surrounded our town on every side. The government, the reports said, planned to cut the forests down, and the photographs the P-38 took would enable the loggers to find the biggest and best and nearest timber.

I read the explanations, but they meant nothing to me. Even if I had understood them, my private imagination of what the plane was and what it was there for was much more compelling. The P-38 was an omen, one that had something to do with baseball. After all, I was on a baseball field the first time it flew over town. And I was on the same field the last time it flew over.

The day after that first flight my friends and I rode our bicycles out to the airport to look the plane over at close quarters, just as we did with every new airplane that appeared. I hid my excitement from my friends and touched the magical fuselage with my hand, reverently breathed in the perfume of its fuel and imagined its heroic war exploits. I felt small and insignificant and capable of almost nothing worthwhile, but I also felt that I was infinitely closer to the realm of the heroic and the magical than I had ever been before.

Yet the moment I touched the magical body of the P-38 my long-standing fantasy about piloting one dissolved. The touch of that metal skin told me that I was touching a very old airplane. It also told me that I wasn't a god, or a king or a hero. I was just a kid trying to play baseball well enough to be chosen for an All-Star team, and I wasn't stupid enough to believe that I would somehow make the All-Star team just because I had touched a P-38 fighter bomber. To make the team I would have to do things that were much more difficult: I would have to field ground balls without making errors, and I would have to overcome my terror of being hit by the ball while I was at bat. So far, I couldn't do those things as well as the two other kids who were trying out for shortstop. This brush with the realm of gods and heroes, I sensed, wouldn't alter who I was or what I was capable of doing.

I watched my friends scramble up on the wings of the aircraft to peer into the cockpit, but I didn't join them. I knew how far it was from the ground where I was, locked in my muddle of ignorance and lack of ability, to that cockpit. Here was beauty, I thought instead, to be observed carefully and from a safe distance. And it was then that I began to examine the plane, and as I did, I noted the evidence of its decay. Here and there along the wings and fuselage were rivets that had come loose, rivets that were rusted, other rivets that were gone altogether. Suddenly, the plane seemed as ancient as the gods themselves must have seemed to Icarus, and as fragile.

"Come on, you guys," I advised my friends. "I don't think you should be fooling around on this plane."

"That's right," agreed a high, clear voice from behind me.

"Nobody is supposed to go near that aircraft."

"Why not?" chorused my friends, beginning to scramble down off the wings of the P-38 without looking to see who was giving them orders.

It was a boy about my age, thin, dark-haired, serious. His name was Jimmie Clark. I'd seen him at school, but he was in a different class. He kept to himself, and he didn't play baseball.

"It's full of photographic equipment," the kid said in a grave voice. "If you jump around on the plane you might put it out of kilter."

"How come you know all that stuff?" I said. "You act like you own this place."

"My father works here. I live just over there," he said, ignoring my sarcasm.

"So where's the pilot of this thing?" demanded one of my friends as all of us crowded around Jimmie Clark in a crude attempt to intimidate him. "Why isn't he here to protect his property?"

"This 'thing' is a P-38 Lightning, and the pilot went into town," answered Jimmie Clark, in the same grave voice that told us he wasn't very intimidated by our antics. "He had something important to do."

Before I could tell him that I knew all about P-38s, he contemptuously turned and walked away from us toward one of the hangars.

We stood and watched him go. There wasn't much else we could do. Airports and aircraft were full of fragile equipment we were far too stupid to understand. If I'd been by myself I might have squatted on the tarmac and waited for the pilot, just to see what a P-38 pilot looked like. But that wasn't to be.

"Let's get back to town," said one of my friends, all of whom, like me, were trying out for the All-Star team. "We've got a practice at three."

•

If the pilot had been around that morning, he would have satisfied my most romantic notion of what a pilot should look like.

He was, I discovered long after that morning, an ex-RAF bomber pilot by the name of Frank Pynn. Over six feet tall, he affected the posture and dress of an adventurer: Clark Gable moustache, fleece-lined flight jacket and a white scarf that trailed behind him whether the wind was blowing or not. He even smoked a pipe.

Getting beneath his romantic facade hasn't been easy. The newspaper reporter who wrote about him at the time was no military historian, and he wasn't much interested in psychology. But as I've pieced together Pynn's personal history, it is clear that the War had left him, like so many flyers, without much in the way of occupational skills, but with a taste for the adventure and danger that had been his everyday fare while he was in Allied Bomber Command. He'd flown over Berlin more than a dozen times, and he claimed to have taken part in the famous Dresden raid.

Frank Pynn must have felt like an orphan after the War was over. He'd come back a hero, but soon found that being a hero isn't an occupation. So he'd drifted around the world, flying a variety of what he still called 'missions'. But these missions were of an increasingly pedestrian nature, and he flew them in aircraft that were becoming more unreliable as each year passed.

There were two more aspects to Pynn's character that need to be mentioned. One of them was that whenever he wasn't flying he drank too much. The second aspect of his character, a harder one to see, was that Frank Pynn was at heart a shy and lonely man. He thought of himself as a failure, even a fake, and consequently he preferred the company of those who either chose not to see through his adventurer's threadbare bluster, or those who couldn't.

Jimmie Clark was one of the latter. His father was the airport's radio operator, an ex-RAF navigator himself who had befriended Pynn until he realized that he was a heavy drinker. Jimmie lived within sight of the runway, and watching planes come and go was a daily preoccupation. The only thing he found more interesting than planes were the men who flew them. To him, Pynn, with his worn flight jacket and swirling scarf, was as extraordinary as the P-38. Consequently, the boy felt honoured when Pynn took a shine to him, explaining the ins and outs of his aircraft to him as if Jimmie were an aviation mechanic, even letting him sit in the cockpit while the engines warmed up. Jimmie's father didn't take it very seriously when his son announced that the great pilot was going to take him up in the P-38. Doing so was against flight regulations and, the father knew, against the policy of the survey company. But he didn't argue with his son over it. Let the boy have his fantasy.

•

The aerial survey took three weeks to complete, finishing early in the afternoon of June 25, 1956. For Pynn it was the end of the job, and he had few prospects. He planned to head east, where some acquaintances were working on a project converting several aging Canso bombers so that they could drop loads of water on forest fires. He would fly the P-38 back to the coast in the morning, pick up his final paycheque and that would be it. He liked the plane, and the thought of giving it up plucked at the veins of sentimentality and resentment that ran equally deep within him.

He hadn't yet packed up at the small hotel he was staying in and, he decided, he needed a drink. He caught a ride into town, packed his bags and took them down to the lobby, where he left them with the desk clerk. There was a small and rowdy bar in the hotel, and he settled in there with a glass of the Scotch whiskey that was one of his many idiosyncratic trademarks. The photographer he'd been working with joined him for a couple of shots, and they talked about the job—how dull it was, and how monotonous the forested landscape was.

"Like the moon," Pynn told his companion glumly. "And about as much interesting life around, too."

As the afternoon wore on Pynn grew more and more morose. It was obvious to him that this small town cared nothing about him and the things he'd done. His resentment began to blend with the Scotch he was putting away to produce an even more sour brew. He didn't like to drink alone, and he'd been drinking alone ever since he arrived three weeks ago. It didn't matter that the photographer drank with him now, and that an occasional logger sat down with him. The loggers all wanted to make stupid jokes at his expense, calling him a flyboy and inviting him to kamikaze this or that.

When he left the bar at six p.m. Pynn appeared perfectly normal. In the lobby he collected his bags and asked the desk clerk to order him a taxi, all without a slurred word. Then he strode outside with a bag under each arm to wait. Several people who saw him pacing back and forth outside the hotel remarked later that he'd seemed agitated, but it was a small town, and unless you took a swing at someone, you were left alone. The cabbie who drove him to the airport said he looked fine.

"He didn't say much," the cabbie added. "Mostly he just gazed out the window as if he was looking for something he'd lost along the side of the road. And he kept counting his fingers as if he was trying to count something that wouldn't stay counted. It was like he had a plan or something, but it kept getting away on him."

What Pynn was mulling over wasn't really a plan. It was more like an itch. He'd felt it before—maybe it'd been there since the war ended. He was trapped, blocked. No matter what he did, which way he turned, it was in front of him, an insurmountable enclosure of boredom and indifference, one that was closing in on him a little each day, squeezing him into something less than he was. He needed to stretch his wings, he needed a mission, and everything in this one-horse town conspired to deny him what he needed.

The taxi let him out at the service hangar. The P-38 stood outside where he'd left it earlier, and as he walked slowly toward it, the itch did become a fuzzy sort of plan. He would show them. He would show these hicks what he was, and what he could do. He would put on a show no one would forget. When he finished with them, every last one of them would know what courage was, and what a good flyer could do with a P-38.

He heard footsteps on the runway behind him.

"You're leaving," a young voice said, heavy with accusation. "You told me you'd take me up before you left."

It was Jimmie Clark. Pynn turned to face him, the white scarf billowing behind him as if it'd been cued.

"I did say I'd take you up, didn't I," he smiled, touching his hand to his forehead, Clark Gable fashion, in a mock salute. "Then take you up I damned well shall. This is your lucky day, my lad."

Pynn couldn't see any reason to make a check of the aircraft. He knew the P-38 intimately—an intimacy that at this moment was joltingly sensuous. The fuel tanks were still partly full from the morning's flight, and the engine was running cleanly.

He helped the boy into the rear cockpit, started the engines and taxied the craft out to the head of the runway. There, abandoning the normal ritual check of the gauges, he called the tower for clearance.

"Clearance for takeoff," Pynn said into the microphone. "One last piece to finish off."

"Roger. Bit late, isn't it?" the voice from the tower crackled in Pynn's headset. It was Jimmie's father. "Thought you were finished."

"Not quite," Pynn answered.

There was a slight pause at the other end. "Cleared for takeoff," the voice said. "Over and out."

Pynn pulled off his headset without acknowledging, except to raise his thumb to Jimmie in the seat behind him.

"Here we go, you bunch of hicks," he said, but not loud enough for Jimmie to hear.

•

Pynn circled the town once, then made his first pass, east-west up the main street of town at 100 feet, lifting the nose of the plane into the afternoon sun at the edge of town. Beneath him he could see that people were stopping to point. He could almost glimpse their startled expressions. He repeated the pass from the opposite direction, coming from out of the sun, then banking sharply to the south around the low hill just southeast of the city centre. Then he flew along the river, bringing the aircraft down to no more than fifteen or twenty feet above the water's murky surface. His next pass was to the northeast, over City Hall and the baseball diamonds. One of the diamonds was dotted with kids.

As he completed the pass, Pynn glanced over his shoulder at his passenger. Jimmie Clark was white-faced, silently trying to hold his composure. He was frightened, and that fear was struggling against his conviction that Pynn was infallible, and that he, Jimmy, was therefore quite safe. Pynn himself was in a state of ecstasy; for the first time in years, he wasn't holding himself back. Beneath him was the pattern of the small town, like so many he'd seen here and in Europe during the war, just an abstract pattern within which tiny, meaningless figures crouched in amazement and terror. Beneath his hands, the rudder: the source of their terror and his power. It felt more substantial than anything had for years.

He circled once more, then made another pass up the main street, this time at tree-top level. Cars stopped and began to pull over, people flattened themselves to the ground or scrambled into doorways. He took the craft up into the eye of the sun, banked it south and made a wide circle. Then he headed the aircraft back at the town, straight for the steep sand cliffs that marked the river and the town's north boundary. The plane felt a little sluggish, and as he dropped down again, he glanced quickly at the fuel gauges. They registered full, which Pynn knew was incorrect. He was distracted from that calculation by a thump as the left wing clipped a treetop, and he responded instinctively, jamming the rudder back and sending the plane into a steep climb. At the top of the climb he held it for a complete loop, coming out of it upside-down no more than fifty feet above the ground. He seemed to be aimed straight at the sand cliffs. Nobody will ever forget this one, he thought, pulling the aircraft sharply up to clear the trees that lined the top of the cliffs.

The P-38 didn't respond as he needed it to. Unknown to him, the wingtanks had been filled while he'd sat drinking in the bar. Pynn had just a second to curse the someone or something he'd cursed daily since the War ended.

•

Two days later I broke the ring-finger on my right hand trying to field a ground ball that seemed to have a mind of its own. I made a big show of how unhappy I was about it, but secretly, I was glad. The moment I saw that flash of flame in the hills I'd realized that I wasn't going to make the All-Star team no matter

66

how hard I tried. The real message my omen had to deliver flared for a instant, dazzlingly public, then disappeared, leaving only a pillar of black smoke rising into the late afternoon sunlight.

My injured hand provided me with a perfect excuse for my failure to become an All-Star. The doctor put an awkward splint across three of my fingers and my mother, as a thoughtful measure to prevent me from trying to play ball anyway, put my right arm in a wonderfully formal sling.

Playing baseball was the furthest thing from my mind. The entire town was buzzing after the excitement of the plane crash, and I was buzzing in my own way along with everyone else. I'd witnessed the miraculous loop. It seemed to me, as it did to everyone else I talked to, that it had been performed directly overhead, for my private illumination. I had also witnessed the explosion that, within seconds, marked the end of the flight. I went over and over it as each new piece of speculation about the crash came to me. I added and subtracted, but the story didn't yield to mathematical logic; something about it wasn't right.

A P-38 had crashed into the hills and two people were dead, one of them the boy who had chased me and my friends off the aircraft weeks before. I, in turn, was injured, and my delight at being fortuitously wounded on the field of combat, even if it was only a baseball field, nevertheless seemed a betrayal of some obscure point of honour I couldn't quite get a hold on.

When the local newspaper came out a few days later, it said that the P-38, flying upside down, clipped a tree as the pilot attempted to fly it through a narrow cut partway up the cliff face. The plane went down in the cut at over 300 miles per hour, filling the shallow ravine with flaming wreckage. Frank Pynn, 38, and Jimmie Clark, 12, died instantly.

The cut in the cliffs obscured the wreckage from sight, and soon a variety of rumours abounded about precisely where the P-38 was, even though most of the town's population had witnessed the crash. There were also some ghoulish rumours that neither of the bodies had been found, or that only certain parts of the bodies had been uncovered amid the wreckage. My friends and I debated whether we should go up and have a look for ourselves, but the thought of coming across some uncollected part of a human body stopped us.

•

The wreckage is still there in that ravine in the hills. The government sent some investigators to the crash site, and they sifted through the wreckage for a week or two, for reasons that nobody in town could quite fathom. As far as the townspeople were concerned, the plane had gone down, two people were dead, too bad, and so let's get on with building this goddamn town. Eventually the investigators went back to wherever they came from, and left the wreckage as it lay. It's almost invisible now, rusted out and covered with moss and rotting tree trunks.

Every once in a while someone tries to locate the site. It's difficult to find, and more often than not the searchers give up without finding it, even though the town—now a city—surrounds the ravine on all sides.

So we are left with the peasants, and their questions. Both change and grow. Sometimes the peasants sicken and die and are replaced by new peasants, but always the questions remain. And to feed themselves each sinks their roots deeper and deeper into the earth, so that tendrils of root and branch obscure the wreckage of past flights, the once-shiny metal bruised and dulled, the wax and feathers and whatever else will easily decompose long since buried and gone. The peasants argue, as they have always done, about whether or not it was possible for such a flight to have taken place. Those who saw it ask themselves why it happened, and a few wonder what it is that moves the silent gods to choose those who fly and crash, and those who watch. And perhaps by that process they learn to wonder if the Labyrinth, which was built to house the awkwardness of human intelligence, is everything we were, and are.

68

Hand Grenade Gary

America still believed in itself in the mid-1950s. It believed in its simple, vigorous soul, and in the courage and rightness of all things American. To us, far to the north in a small Canadian town just newly connected to the rest of our own country by roads and by radio stations, America was a fantasy, the source of exotic merchandise that occasionally fell into our greedy hands. Nestled as we were amongst a series of mountain ranges, radio reception was poor, and television was still a few years and six hundred miles away. And so was the rest of the global village we all live in now, with its hyperactive impulse to communicate to us about its glittering consumer products, and the bizarre isolations both product and communication have wreaked on the human community.

When the roads improved, the Americans began to bring it to us. They came in person: loud-talking, hand-shaking, big-spending overweight men driving camper trucks that had vast amounts of equipment strung across them, built into them, crammed inside of them. These first Americans all looked like Ernest Hemingway. Only a few of us knew who Ernest Hemingway was, and those book-reading souls who had read his stories lamented that our visitors didn't act much like Hemingway, who they said was, above all, a man of great formality and ferocious honour.

But the children among us liked the Americans well enough. They did strange and flamboyant things. They spent money as if they were practising a religion, showing the bland greenbacks to us if we asked, and when we amused them, they gave us shiny American coins that told us they trusted in God. More than that, they seemed to trust in the powerful guns they fondled and brandished in public. But they did not know, as our fathers all did, how to hunt with these guns, and they did not seem to care. Money and guns were their way of doing things, part of their being, part of their brotherhood. And above all else, the Americans believed in the idea of brotherhood.

"This is a big world and we're all part of it," they said. "America is a state of mind. It's big and it's powerful and it's pretty damned decent. The Arsenal of Democracy."

From my social studies books at school I'd already learned all about Woodrow Wilson and the Roosevelt brothers and the Arsenal of Democracy. And now, here it was, in my own home town.

Having made their speeches about brotherhood, the Americans did not wait for us to ask a lot of questions. No sir. Americans take certain truths to be self-evident, and the greatest and most self-evident of these is that all men are brothers. Americans are big brothers to the world, and all non-Americans are their younger, weaker and slightly backward brothers.

We didn't have any philosophical questions for them anyway. The merchants had already begun to refer to them as an Important Industry, and that sort of talk carried more weight than the few remarks from wiseacres who said that any country that had so many camper trucks full of rich shitheads must indeed be the arsehole of democracy.

No one thought of saying "Yankee Go Home". On the contrary, most people went out of their way to make the visitors feel at home, which is to say they gladly took their American money. In exchange the Americans took the trout we had more than enough of and shot the abundant moose and the grizzlies that were so

70

numerous they were like pests. Their excesses for the most part seemed a careless sort of largesse.

As a nation the Americans had succeeded in defeating every enemy they'd chosen to confront. Just recently they'd squashed Hitler and the Japanese, and after that was done, they'd pushed the Commies back inside their own boundaries in Korea. We'd helped them do it, they generously admitted; we were therefore Semi-Americans and if, as individuals, they wanted to come up here and defeat some Nature, like Ernest Hemingway did, well, wasn't that great? Who could object? No one I knew objected, and so neither did I. I went off to the library and read up on Ernest Hemingway.

•

Hand Grenade Gary had been an instrumental part of every defeat America had inflicted on its enemies in his lifetime. He was a grizzled, overweight, and immensely wealthy California businessman. He'd been in the U.S. Marines, and every time he introduced himself, which he did to just about everyone he met—man, woman or young boy—he named the marine division, regiment, and the squad of men he'd headed.

Gary took pride in never getting second best. He owned the most powerful hunting rifles, drove the loudest, most over equipped camper, and spent the most money. He flew floatplanes into the most sheltered of our lakes to fish for trout; he rented helicopters to reach the most remote of our mountain meadows to shoot grizzly and sheep. He also had the distinction of being the only American we ever saw who carried a loop of hand grenades on his belt.

The grenades quickly made him a legend, particularly with us kids. Whenever his bright red camper stopped in town, we crowded around it. Gary found himself being mobbed by bright-eyed children demanding to look at his grenades, asking if they were real, and would he please set one off to show what they could do.

"Well, now," he'd say. "These here ordinance are highly lethal weapons. I can't go around wasting them to amuse a bunch of kids."

71

Then he'd pull out a fat cigar, hand the empty metal tube to the nearest lucky kid, irrumate the cigar and, using a Zippo lighter with the U.S. Marine insignia on both sides, light it.

"You never know when you're gonna need a grenade," he'd say, taking a giant puff and filling the air with blue smoke. "But if you can find me some Commies maybe I'll show you what one of these babies can do."

We looked all over the place for Commies, but there weren't any. When we'd tell him that the next time we saw him, he'd laugh long and loud.

"Well," he'd say, "that's one of the reasons I like it around here."

•

For a few years, Gary did a good job of being a legend, driving up from California with his hand grenades each autumn to hunt and fish and drink whiskey. But his whole world blew up on him one September, and a small part of ours came apart with it. He bought himself a riverboat trip up one of the wildest rivers in the north, travelling as a special passenger in a convoy of the big narrow boats that were then the only means of transporting freight through the isolated reaches of the Rocky Mountain trench. During the trip, something happened: two men, native Indians, were killed and Gary was charged with the killings.

It took a while for the story to come clear, and even when it did some people denied that it was true, although I noticed that the ones who were saying it was a lie were the ones who were making a lot of money from the American tourists.

On the way up the river, the story went, one of the boats broke up in a particularly savage stretch of rapids, and Gary refused to help in salvaging the equipment that went overboard. Of course he was forced to help—on the riverboats nobody could be a spectator—but while they were attempting to pick up the outboard motor and some other equipment that had lodged itself precariously on some rocks, Gary let go of a rope and all of it was swept away.

The captain of the boat, an Indian who'd spent his life on the

72

river, said something to Gary, and a fist fight ensued. Gary lost the fight—some say honestly, and others say because two or three of the riverboat men put it to him. Whatever the truth was, that night Gary tossed a grenade into the tent where the riverboat captain was sleeping. The explosion killed the captain and another man. A third man lost a leg.

When the riverboats came out several days later, Gary was taken to the police station, tied with ropes and covered with bruises, and despite the wranglings of some slick-eyed lawyers who flew in all the way from California, he was charged with manslaughter. But the lawyers did manage to get him released on bail the same day. Most people expected him to skip town, and that would be the end of the matter, and of Gary.

But Gary didn't leave town. On the contrary, he hung around town bragging about how no court would touch him—he was an American citizen, after all, and as he put it, "what's a few Indians worth, anyhow?"

He even parked his camper in the parking lot behind the Courthouse and held his own kind of court there, offering free beer to all comers and partying halfway through the night the week before the trial.

The police left him alone. At least, they said, this way they knew where to find him. But when the trial began, nearly everyone else left him alone too, except the town drunks.

The trial didn't go the way Gary thought it would. The riverboat men angrily stuck to their story, saying some ugly things about Gary and what he'd done on the river. There was even an editorial in the newspaper about the 'Democracy of the River', and how the accused didn't seem to understand that on the river no one cared who you were or what your racial background was as long as you were good with the boats and paid attention to the rules of the river.

After three days of testimony, the jury went into seclusion to make their decision, and Gary went out to the parking lot and locked himself in the back of his camper. Some of his American cronies and the few local followers he had left tried to coax him out, but Gary wouldn't talk to them.

The jury came back in after less than an hour, and the court bailiff was sent out to summon Gary to the courtroom to receive the verdict. He knocked on the camper door, but Gary wouldn't open up. Instead, he opened one of the louvred windows of the camper and told everyone to stand clear, and a few seconds later, Gary's grenades blew him and the camper to smithereens.

After the mess was cleaned up and the Coroner's inquest held, a strange argument passed through the city. I heard about it from my father, who'd never been one of Gary's fans. Some people, he said, claimed that Gary was laughing in the back of that truck before he pulled the pins on those grenades of his. Others claimed that he was crying.

"If what he was doing in there was laughing," one of the local guys who was there told my father, "I'd have hated to see the man cry."

I didn't know what to think. Whenever I'd seen Hand Grenade Gary he looked like he had everything figured out, but that must have been a lie. I wondered about Ernest Hemingway too, because he wrote as if he had everything in his boat tied down tight. I found myself wondering how he'd have made out with those riverboaters, and if things would have gone any differently than they did with Gary. My father advised me to forget about Ernest Hemingway, and told me to steer clear of 'those Yankees.'

After Gary blew himself up, people around town cooled a little toward Americans. They didn't stop coming up, though. In fact, every year there seemed to be more of them. But there was somehow less talk about brotherhood, and they didn't hang around town quite as much. My father said they were only interested in killing our biggest moose and grizzly and catching our biggest fish so they could be turned into the trophies Americans needed to prove they were men.

One time he told me that the Americans would have more fun if they'd relax a little more and quit pretending they were the best at everything. "But then, I suppose if they did," he said, gesturing at the new buildings sprouting all over the town, "none of this would be happening, and we'd still be out in the middle of nowhere. There would be," he shrugged, "no America."

The World Machines

Around noon on my nineteenth birthday, Old Man Nelson showed up at the small shack I lived in. I heard him coming, talking to himself as usual, and I opened the door as he reached for the doorknob. He would have walked in without knocking, just like most people. With him I didn't mind—he owned the land my shack stood on, and he'd never once asked me to pay any rent.

"Put your coat on, son," he said in his slight Scandinavian accent. "I got something you need to know about. It's your birthday present."

Old Man Nelson drove a huge black Oldsmobile that looked like a gangster's car. But he didn't look like a gangster. He looked like what he was: a retired logger who'd made a lot of money and who told stories about everything under the sun except how he'd made his money. I don't remember how I got to know him, but since I liked to listen to his stories and I lived on one of the many properties he owned, we came as close as young men and old men come to real friendship. For a couple of years, I spent quite a lot of time listening to him.

"You know," he began, as he turned the big Oldsmobile out of the alley, "them buggers who run things don't do it by themselves, eh?"

He knew this question would interest me because we frequently talked about how things were run around the city. I'd noticed, among other things, that even though the Mayor and Council of our small town were stupid and short-sighted men, they exercised a degree of authority and control they couldn't possibly have understood and certainly didn't earn. There was a kind of gap between what they said about how things worked and the complex and overlapping processes by which even I could see the city operated. This gap, which I merely sensed without understanding its workings, was a disturbing darkness that resided at the core of the city. I could never quite forget that it was there.

I began to see it while I was a small boy, watching the city crews dig up the streets, install pipes in the holes, and then fill in the holes. The next year they would do the same thing over again. One year it was water pipes. The next year, sewer pipes. Another year, gas. Then they replaced the pipes. I believed, as most children do, that the world and every action in it had a purpose; that it was under some sort of benevolent and rational control, even though I'd already begun to realize there was very little evidence to back this up. Watching the crazy way the crews dug up the streets every year convinced me, by itself, that whatever was going on wasn't rational or benevolent on any terms I could understand, but I continued to believe at least it operated on some sort of logic. But what was that logic, and what did it serve? As I grew older, finding the answer to that question preoccupied me, and consequently, Old Man Nelson's opener snapped me to attention.

"What do you mean, they don't do it by themselves?"

Old Man Nelson had a way of telling stories that made things fuzzier before it made them clear. That was one of the reasons I liked listening to his anecdotes and stories. Listening to them was like walking into a fog and coming out with money in my pocket. All I had to do was show some curiosity, then nod my head in the right places to assure him that I was listening carefully. He'd talk, and I'd generally learn something interesting or useful.

"Well," he said slowly, "those buggers don't know much of anything. They just know where the switches are, and they like having people running this way and that more than they should."

I nodded, but kept silent. It made sense, but this wasn't the right time to question. I let the fog spread.

"Out by the lake I'll show you something you've never seen before," he said.

I'd been to the lake dozens of times, and I'd never seen anything unusual, except maybe the time my sister got a bloodsucker up her nose.

"You've never seen it because you didn't expect anything unusual to be there," he said, fielding my unasked question perfectly. "That's the way these guys do things. They put things where nobody expects them to be, and so nobody looks right at them. You can't see what anything is unless you look right at it. Even then what you're seeing can't be understood if you don't have the words to get a hold on it."

"Who's 'they'?" I asked. We shared a taxonomy but our vocabularies were slightly different. For instance, Old Man Nelson called the mayor and coucil 'them buggers'. I referred to them as 'those assholes'. Maybe the difference was because they really hadn't done anything to me yet, and Old Man Nelson often complained that they spent most of their energy thinking up ways to screw him.

"The bosses," he said.

"You mean those assholes down at City Hall?"

"No. Them buggers don't know nothing. I mean the big bosses." He paused. "The ones you never see. If you're really doing something you don't go strutting around like a rooster, crowing about it."

"So what do these big bosses do, anyway?"

"They run everything, and they make sure nobody gets out."

I sat in the roomy imitation leather seat beside Old Man Nelson and watched the shacks whiz by outside the car window, mulling over the idea. I wondered for a moment if he was talking about God, and decided he wasn't. He didn't believe in that crap, and neither did I, any more. The idea of God used to be comforting. This idea wasn't. I didn't know a lot, but I had figured out that anyone with that kind of power wasn't going to be interested in me. Power was for assholes, and I didn't want to be an asshole. I didn't know what I wanted to be, but I knew that there were a lot of assholes out there, that the world was full of assholes, and that the world seemed to be changing in such a way that only assholes would be able to get anywhere in it. Old Man Nelson was about the only adult I knew who wasn't an asshole, come to think of it.

"You asleep?" he asked, as much to prevent me from falling asleep as anything.

I could sleep anywhere, any time, without the slightest provocation. I think he admired that talent more than anything else about me. He often said that if he didn't talk to me constantly I'd drop off on him. Then he'd laugh and tell me to get lots of sleep now, because when I got old like him I wouldn't ever get any sleep. He didn't sleep much, he said, because he knew too much, and if he let his guard down, them buggers would walk all over him.

"I'm not sleepy today," I said. "What did you mean when you said the bosses run everything?"

Old Man Nelson paused, as if figuring out a way to make it simple enough for me to understand. Whenever he was thinking hard an odd expression came over his face, a grin that made him look part goat and part elf. "People get up in the morning and then they sleep most of the night, right?"

"Right." I didn't bother to complicate things by pointing out that he didn't sleep that way.

"Why?" he asked flatly.

"What do you mean, why?" I replied. "Because that's how things work. You can't stay awake all the time. If you tried, you'd get too tired to stay awake, and then..." I sensed that I was digging myself into a hole. "Darkness makes people sleepy," I finished lamely. "I dunno."

"If everybody got up when they wanted to, and slept when they wanted to, the bosses' system would get buggered up," he said. "Some people would sleep all the time, like you, and some would sleep all day and stay up all night, and some people wouldn't sleep at all."

78

"I guess."

"And things would start to change."

"Yeah?" I said, starting to see some shapes in the fog. For one thing, I was going to have to revise my theory about change. Instead of changing things, the bosses were keeping things as they were.

"Yeah. So the bosses keep it all going the way it already is."

"If everybody did what they wanted wouldn't everything just break down?"

Old Man Nelson gazed at me patiently. "At first, that's about all it would be. But after a while people would start seeing what really needs to be done, and when that happened, things would start to change."

"So how do the bosses keep things from changing?"

"That's what I'm going to show you," he said.

"So what you're saying is that the bosses don't want anything to change, and that's a bad thing, is that it?"

"Sure. They don't want real change, anyway. Things in the city can grow bigger, like trees do, and if they grow bigger people think things are changing when they're not. But if something different—really different—starts to happen then the bosses might lose."

"Might lose what?"

"I dunno. I've never figured out what it is they're so damned scared of losing. Money, maybe, but maybe something more."

"Something more?" I asked. "Like what?"

Old Man Nelson shook his head. "You wouldn't understand if I told you."

"How come you know all this?" I asked. "Is it because you don't sleep much yourself?"

Old Man Nelson thought that one through before he answered. I felt the car slow down.

"I dunno about that either," he said, finally. "I guess I got a funny ticker in me. Damn thing doesn't work like it's supposed to. I keep waking up with my heart pumping like a pack of dogs chasing a rabbit, and I start seeing things."

The car speeded up again, and I watched the shacks along the roadside get blurry until they seemed like one, long, continuous shack. They began to peter out, and for a while, all there was to look at were blurred birch and poplar thickets.

As we started up the long ridge that overlooked the lake, the countryside started to change. The trees got larger, and, I noticed for the first time, more evenly spaced. Old Man Nelson was whistling quietly. The tune was unfamiliar, but catchy. We reached the crest of the ridge, and I could see the brilliant blue water of the lake below.

"Down we go," said Old Man Nelson, and abruptly pulled the car off the main road, through a shallow thicket of willows and onto a narrow paved lane I didn't know was there. For a second I thought he'd gone crazy and was smashing up the car. We'd been going at least fifty miles per hour.

"Not many people know about this road," he said, as if that explained his peculiar method of entering it.

"I sure didn't," I whispered, beginning to breathe again as he slowed down.

I couldn't see the lake anywhere, and it should have been easily visible as soon as we pulled off the main highway. The lane we were slipping silently along was strange. I could see it hadn't been used much, because the tarmac was still clean and black. The underbrush crowded closely along it, and in places had begun to infringe on the margins. I didn't know what to make of it, and I sat there, expecting the lake to appear any second. But it didn't, and Old Man Nelson kept driving.

Then the underbrush along the sides of the lane thinned out and disappeared, and the evergreens went with it. The evergreens were replaced by geometrically spaced poplars, their pale olive-green trunks unspotted and straight. The lane flattened out, and seemed to turn back on itself. I felt panic rising in me; I'd heard the stories about old men kidnapping people and killing them, although I couldn't really relate those stories to Old Man Nelson. As if to reassure me, he chuckled to himself and told me it was just a little farther.

The lane curved through the poplars again, and ended abruptly in a small clearing. At the head of the clearing the ground rose sharply and there was something like the front of a building cut into the hill. It was odd-looking, constructed as an arch with two pillars about twenty feet high on each side of the doors. The doors themselves were glass, like the kind they put in supermarkets. They even had the recessed rubber mats in front of them that make the doors open automatically.

Old Man Nelson brought the Oldsmobile to a halt at the far edge of the clearing, and I stepped out into a field of plants. They were flowering, and I recognized them as Indian paintbrushes. Like the poplars, they were native to the area, and like the poplars they had obviously been planted in a rigid geometry that made them seem as foreign as they should have been familiar. Then I remembered that it was still early summer, and that Indian paint-brushes bloomed much later in the year, in August.

"They're smart sons-of-bitches," Old Man Nelson said as I knelt down to pick one of the red flowers. "They get them to bloom right from the time they come up out of the snow until freeze-up. But they don't taste good like the real ones do."

I pulled one of the nectar tubes from the flower and sucked the transparent liquid from it. It tasted bitter and I spat it out.

"You should listen to me better," Old Man Nelson laughed. "Let's go inside and I'll show you some things."

He walked toward the glass doors and sure enough, they opened when he stepped on the rubber mat. We went inside and I followed him down a dim corridor.

"What is this place?" I asked, the questions bubbling out of me involuntarily. "Who owns it? Are you sure we're supposed to be in here?"

"You ask too many questions all at once, and none of them are the right ones," he answered, his voice echoing along the corridor.

"Who built this place?" I continued, searching for the right question without any idea of what it was or how to find it. "How long have you known about it? Does everybody know about it? How long are we going to be in here? Do you know the people who run this? Do you know how to get out of here?"

"Wrong questions, wrong questions!" answered Old Man Nelson, waving his hands but not stopping to turn around.

I gave up and followed him silently down the dim corridor. The walls moved back, and above me in the gloom I could just

81

barely make out a network of steel pipes that stretched out and up in both directions. Here and there the network was penetrated by steel walkways and platforms, each with an array of wheel valves, switches and small coloured lights. From the low even hum I knew that whatever the installation was, it was working, operating. What it was doing, I had no clue.

Except for Old Man Nelson and me, it was deserted. I was lagging behind—for an elderly man, Old Man Nelson walked swiftly, certainly, and I found myself scrambling to stay up with him. When I got even with him, I caught at his sleeve.

"What is this place?" I asked, almost pleading. "Where are we going?"

Old Man Nelson gazed at me without slowing his pace, and without answering my questions. As I grabbed at his sleeve again, he swerved out of my grasp and into an alcove I hadn't seen. He stopped, and waited for me to enter behind him.

"Wait," he whispered. "We can't talk here."

I obeyed, and found myself following him down a long, narrow corridor with a low ceiling. Up ahead I could see that the corridor ended in a set of glass doors much like the ones we'd come in by.

Old Man Nelson stepped on the rubber mat, the doors opened, and he walked through them into a room that was instantly flooded with bright light. I followed, skipping into a run to keep the doors from closing against me.

"We can talk here," he said calmly.

The flood of my questions washed over him until he waved me back.

"I'll start from the beginning," he said. "This installation is one of their machines. I don't know for sure how large it is. Very large, obviously. It isn't the only one I've seen either. I discovered another one, smaller and not so fancy, years ago, just before I left the Old Country."

"What is it for?" I asked. "Who built it?"

"The bosses built it," said Old Man Nelson. "They built it to prevent us from changing the way things are. They keep them hidden to prevent people from finding them and understanding what they're doing. If people found out how much of their lives were controlled they might tear them down."

"But we're here," I said. "You found two of them, and now you're showing me this one."

"Hah!" he scoffed. "You're gonna see how much difference that makes. I've been trying to show this thing to people for thirty years now, and you're the first one I got to see it."

"Thirty years? I'm the first one?" I felt equally tempted by both questions.

"I took my own boys out here but they just laughed at me. They couldn't see what I was talking about."

I knew he had three sons, and that he didn't have much use for any of them. Two were already wealthy logging contractors, and the third was at some big university back east studying to be a lawyer. Old Man Nelson's criticism of them was always the same: 'too goddamn busy making money to see what the money was making them into.'

"You're saying that this thing has been here for thirty years?" I asked, not quite believing that it could have been. It looked new, and from the entrance, very modern.

"I only said I've *known* about it for thirty years," he said, smiling at me as if I should know better. "It wasn't this big when I first found it."

"How big is it?"

Old Man Nelson scratched his chin just as if he were trying to decide how far it was to the corner store.

"I walked it out this way, a few years ago," he said, pointing in the direction we'd been going. "I figure it goes almost all the way to the river, which is about nine miles. Down at the far end you can hear the river if you put your ear to the wall. The last time I checked it didn't go as far to the north, but then that was where the newest machinery was, so I don't know how much it's grown."

"What does it do?" I asked, after a moment of silence.

"I can't answer that for you," he said. "I can show you what it is, but I can't tell you what it does, exactly."

I waited for him to explain what he meant by that, but he didn't elaborate. Another silence ensued, but it wasn't, I realized, really silent. Beneath our voices was the sound of the machine, which alternated regularly between a deep rumble and a drone-like hum.

"Can we go farther in," I asked, "so I can figure it out for myself?"

"We could," he said, "but it wouldn't help you. Besides, there's a danger I might lose track of you, and I don't know if you could get out on your own."

"Can we try to go farther anyway?"

"You can always try," he said, his tone shifting, as we were suddenly discussing another matter. "But it's the same here as anywhere else. You'll reach a place where you're not capable of taking in what you're seeing, and when that point is reached you stop being able to understand. If you can't understand things, you come under their control. That's no good. You've got to take this in a little at a time."

I didn't understand what was going on and I didn't really understand much of what he was saying, and instinctively I began to look around me for something material that would enable me to. He lapsed into silence, and I turned and sidled over to examine one of the walls of the room. When I touched it, it was utterly smooth, undefined, although from a distance it had appeared to be rough concrete. I jerked my hand back, alarmed.

"It's like that," he said. "That's the frightening part. From a distance, it seems to make sense, and it can almost look familiar. But the closer you come to it the less definition it has. That's one of the ways you recognize their materials."

"Are there other entrances?"

"Lots of them. They're all over the place, but it's difficult to recognize what they are when you see them. The one we entered by is the only one I know how to reach. I guess you could say that it belongs to me."

"Are you here a lot? I mean, do you spend very much of your time in here?"

Old Man Nelson sighed. "You better start to watch your language more carefully. I don't 'spend' time—that's their way of thinking. I lose time here, but I don't spend it, because I get nothing back, and neither does anyone else. And I'm here a lot. More and more as the years go on."

I wasn't used to fluorescent lights, and my eyes were getting sore. Worse, I was having trouble breathing. The room—and the whole installation—was air-conditioned, but all that did was to flavour the air with an acrid dustiness. I wanted to get out, but I also wanted to find out as much as I could about the place.

"Where are we now?" I asked, gesturing at the walls around us. "What is this room?"

"It's sort of a museum," Old Man Nelson replied with an ironic chuckle. "I've found a few of them like this. The only difference between this and the rest of the installation is that out there, anything resembling a question and answer sequence activates the control panels. In here, as far as I can tell, nothing happens. That's why I brought you here to answer your questions."

"How'd you find out about that if you've never brought anyone else here?"

"I didn't say that. I said that no one else has been able to see what it is. You should listen more carefully." He took my arm and pushed me gently in the direction of the doors. I balked.

"One more question?"

"Okay, ask it. But no more."

"I don't understand how this can be a museum. There's nothing here except bright lights and walls I can't see properly. Museums are supposed to be full of relics, dead things. This place is more like a waiting room."

"This is a museum at least on the bosses' terms. A museum, as far as they're concerned, is just a warehouse to store dangerous substances in, a place where things or ideas are put in order to make them inactive. Does that answer your question?"

It didn't, but I nodded anyway. "I guess so," I said.

I followed him back down the corridor and into the larger cavern with its overhead array of pipes. Old Man Nelson turned back the way we'd come. I wanted to see more, so I quietly slipped off in the opposite direction. I was hoping that by the time he noticed, I'd be so far away he'd have to let me go on by myself. There was nothing about the installation that was frightening to me now. Already it seemed familiar and dull, and it didn't feel like I was in any physical danger. After all, the place was empty except for the two of us, and the machinery far above my head, humming steadily.

I walked several hundred yards without looking behind me, and heard nothing from Old Man Nelson. When I turned around to see if he was coming after me, he'd vanished. That didn't alarm me. I knew roughly where I was, and getting out was simply a matter of following the long corridor back to the entrance where, no doubt, Old Man Nelson would be waiting.

I walked, the sound of my footsteps lost beneath the hum, for what felt like several miles. But the landscape around me, if that's what it was, stayed the same. Then, among the gun-metal grey of the pipes overhead appeared other colours: at first pastels, and then richer primary colours. The effect was of a riot of colour. I was gazing up into them when I bumped into Old Man Nelson.

"Are you impressed?" he asked.

"With what? With all this?"

"With the colour," he laughed. "Do you know where you are?"

Until that moment I thought I knew where I was. But since I had no idea how Old Man Nelson had gotten there, I was no longer so sure. Without waiting for my answer, he took me by the arm and walked me through a set of automatic glass doors. I was startled to find myself outside the entrance we'd entered by.

Old Man Nelson didn't offer any explanation. He just told me to get into the car.

"It's getting late," he said gruffly, as if he regretted the entire episode. "I've got some things I have to take care of."

Overhead, the sky had clouded over, and the poplars were shimmering in the light breeze, exposing the silvery undersides of their leaves like they always do before it rains.

•

But it didn't rain that afternoon. It should have, but since that afternoon, nothing else has been the way it should be, or the way it used to be. We drove back to town on the dusty gravel roads. Old Man Nelson didn't have much to say and neither did I. He dropped me off at the shack and as I got out of the big black car I thanked him for showing me the machines. He just laughed in a preoccupied sort of way.

"You don't have to thank me for that," he said. "The buggers

86

were there all the time. Now you gotta figure out what they are, and how to remember what they are. After that, you'll have to decide what you're going to do about them.''

•

I knew exactly what to do. Those machines were composed of pipes and there was network of pipes in the ground all through the city. Obviously, they were connected. I turned my small shack upside-down trying to find where they entered. Then I realized that my place wasn't like most—I had no running water, no toilet, no gas. I checked the electrical system, but found nothing unusual except a third bare copper wire that seemed to have no purpose.

For weeks after that, I drove everyone I knew crazy as I checked their houses for pipes. I found apparently disconnected pipes and irrelevant wires everywhere I looked, but I couldn't establish a pattern to any of it, no logic. I gave up when my mother, after eyeing me carefully while I searched her house, suggested that perhaps I should see a doctor about my problem.

•

That August, Old Man Nelson died. I didn't get to see very much of him after he showed me the machines. He just didn't come around. I wanted to go out to see the machines again, but we didn't have the kind of friendship that allowed me to visit him. He'd always come by on his own time, and now he didn't seem to have much of it for me. It was as if he were in a hurry, all of a sudden. He told me himself that he was busy—'planning something important', he said when I ran into him on a downtown street one hot afternoon. He looked tired, older than before, his step slower, his breathing laboured. I didn't think too much about it because his eyes were as bright and alert as ever—maybe more so.

I had a hard time finding out the exact details of his death. His wife didn't like me, and because his sons knew the old man preferred my company to theirs, they didn't like me either. I sent a note when I heard about his death, but nobody answered it. I even phoned his wife. But since I didn't really know what I

87

wanted to ask her, and she was aggressively not interested in talking to me about anything, our conversation was a short one. From what I was able to piece together, Old Man Nelson organized a family reunion of some sort—all his sons were in town before he died, and so were a number of relatives. The reunion—a picnic—was held at the lake less than a mile from the stretch of road where he'd pulled the car through that thicket to show me the entrance to the machine.

At the picnic, the old man had attempted to take the family for a walk in the woods. When they refused to go with him, he flew into a rage, storming off deliberately, according to his son, into one of the impenetrable alder and devil's club thickets that surround the lake.

When he didn't come back, a search was launched. They found him in a small clearing at the heart of the thicket. At first they thought he was sleeping, his head cradled comfortably on a mossy log amid the Indian paintbrushes that filled the clearing. The paintbrushes were in full bloom, but the old man was dead. His wife said that it was his heart.

I went to the funeral, even though I knew Old Man Nelson had been a vocal atheist. A preacher got up and had a few things to say about the life beyond, and how, although he didn't know 'the deceased', as he put it, he was certain that Old Man Nelson was going to his deserved reward. None of the sons delivered a eulogy, and there weren't very many people there, considering Old Man Nelson had lived in the town for close to fifty years. I didn't go to the interment, and the family didn't hold a wake. They all looked impatient during the service, like they were needed elsewhere.

I hitch-hiked out to the lake a few days later. The man who gave me the ride thought I was a bit nuts, wanting to get out on a stretch of deserted highway, particularly since it was fire season and a small fire was burning in some slash only two or three miles away.

"You never know when those fires can take off with the wind and burn off a whole goddamned hillside," he told me.

"Not this one," I replied, and slammed the car door shut, waving him on.

I found the lane easily; it was simply "there", as if it had been waiting for me. But as I walked down the gently sloping tarmac, I sensed a change: the poplars were losing their leaves, and as I reached the turn where before the trees had grown in regimented order across the flattened park-like landscape, instead of order I saw carnage: trees with broken tops, trees blown down, and here and there between them, mounds of debris: old house siding, bits of stucco, broken bottles, scraps of pastel plastic. In the clearing where the glass doors with the columns had been, there was a sizeable gravel pit, the bottom covered with about two feet of slimy water rhinestoned with gasoline and diesel. The air was rife with the stink of garbage and petroleum.

The entrance to the machine itself was different. The glass doors had been removed and in their place were heavy steel doors of the same gun-metal grey of the first pipes I'd seen inside. The rubber mats were gone, and so were the columns.

I tried the door, and it opened—not automatically, and not easily—but it did open. I hesitated, not sure if it was safe to enter, and as I did so I heard a familiar laugh. I spun around, and there, just beyond the gravel pit, I thought I caught a glimpse of Old Man Nelson disappearing into an alder thicket.

I hurtled after him, down into the pit and through the scummy water, and up the slope into the thicket. But there was nothing there but the trees. Not a thing moved but the dappled sunlight filtering through the trees. I stood still for a moment, and then my ears picked up the faintest hum. In front of me was a clearing, and as if what the old man showed me had never been, the Indian paintbrushes bloomed in honeyed disarray beneath the smoky August sun. I sat down among them and waited. The hum grew louder, and I remembered that I'd left the doors to the cavern open.

The Deer Park

My name is August Jensen. I've been thinking about what I'm going to tell you for fifty years, ever since the day I stumbled onto the place. Between then and now I can't remember one day that's gone by without it coming up on me in one way or another. It's been my life, really.

I don't have long to live. It's my liver, and there's nothing the doctors can do to keep me going. I'm not complaining, mind you. Everybody has to die, and I've had more years than most, and I've had fewer tears and fewer hardships than a lot of good people I've known. What I'm saying is, I've had a decent life, and I have no complaints about my lot.

When the doctor came in and told me, in his roundabout way, I felt something akin to relief. I've been a solitary man for most of the last fifty years, and I believe I've had reason to be that way.

It isn't that I haven't had friends. I've had many, and for the most part they've been honest and loyal, which is all a man can ask. Lord knows, even still one or two come to visit me every week I'm here.

But for fifty years I've been keeping a secret. For many of those years I didn't want to think about it, and I guess it poisoned a part of me. When I did think about it, it seemed to me that I might be insane; or even worse, cursed. I decided not to marry for that reason. I have no children, and when I die my line will die with me. I want no immortality.

For many years I hoped to forget about the things I saw, but there's been no relief from them. They've remained untarnished and clear; and keeping them bottled up has exhausted me more than the passing years have. I tell you, no one can comprehend the incomprehensible.

So here I am on my deathbed scratching this down. I can only tell you what it is that I've seen, what I think I saw, and the small portion of it I can understand.

•

There had always been rumours about a strange island up the river, but like most people, I thought they were a jimcrack of native legend, childish fantasy and cabin-fever. I heard the rumours when I was very young, but no one else seemed interested. My older brothers told me the rumours were like those stories about elves, goblins and fairies: pleasant enough, but nonsense. Yet there was an obvious difference, and I often wondered why nobody noticed it. The elves and fairies were from never-never land—at best they originated far off, in old Europe. The stories about the island all agreed on one point: the island was supposed to be no more than forty miles upriver from town.

That was the first strange thing. No one went there, or if they did, they didn't talk about what they'd seen. I was no more than a lad of, say, twelve years when I figured that out. I'd decided that if there was a strange island a few miles from town, it should be easy to find someone who'd seen it. I started to search for eyewitnesses. Well, there were none, believe me, none willing to talk. Most of the old-timers shied away from the subject, telling me that no boats went up that way. There was nothing up there, they said, but bad water and bugs.

They were correct, for the most part. The surrounding country, all the way into the mountains, was the worst kind of muskeg. The railroad went through there, but that was because it had to. The few settlements in the area existed only to log the patches of timber that weren't scrub spruce and cottonwood. The loggers cut the trees, dumped them into the river, and pulled them out again just short of town. The men who worked out there stayed in temporary camps, coming and going on the railroad, never staying long enough to explore the river or the surrounding countryside.

My father travelled through that country in the early days, but he was a logger himself. There was better timber elsewhere, he said, and left it at that.

Maybe it was my curiosity that led me to become a surveyor and not a logger. That's what I did for a living. I worked in virgin country laying down survey lines for the government. In those days most loggers didn't live very long, and if they did, it was usually because they were crippled by the work instead of being killed by it.

As a surveyor, I was able to keep my health, and I got to see some of the prettiest country in this part of the world while it was still clean and untouched. Over the years I surveyed a good part of the north, travelling by foot or canoe, and later on by motorized riverboats and float planes. I made a decent living, and except for a few scars that were the result of my own carelessness, my body and mind have remained more or less intact.

I was almost thirty years old before my work carried me upriver on a government survey, one of the first attempts to chart the upper reaches of the river since Sir Alexander Mackenzie came through at the end of the eighteenth century. What I saw there isn't documented in any survey, and the maps I made show nothing unusual. But I don't think I should pass on without making some record of what I saw and heard, and of what it did to me and the men I took with me.

My companions on the survey were Angus MacKay, a dour Scotsman ten years my senior, and a Métis lad by the name of Jimmie Paquette. Despite MacKay's greater age, I was the survey chief. Not that he was lacking in the qualities that make for a good woodsman and surveyor. He was competent, courageous and not lacking in intelligence. But he was drinker and a womanizer, and not trusted by the outfitters or anyone in a position of authority. But he'd led one of my earliest surveys and when he came to me looking for work as my assistant, I didn't hesitate. In the bush he was one of the best, and a good companion to boot. What he did in town was his own affair.

Jimmie Paquette was neither overly bright nor skilled in the bush, despite his native background. But he had a strong back, and he did what he was told without complaint. It might be said that when it counted, his will was stronger than mine or that of the stout MacKay, and without Jimmie I might not be here to tell my story. But I'm getting ahead of myself.

•

We embarked on our survey early in the morning on the 23rd of June, 1932, well after the waters had crested. Our outfit consisted of a twenty-five foot riverboat, locally made, equipped with a single kicker. The area we were commissioned to survey was the thirty-mile stretch east of the mouth of the McGregor river, and the country to the north up to the Monkman range and the Arctic Divide at Pacific Lake, close to 900 square miles in all.

It was at the end of the first day, after moving upriver on the Fraser against a swift but smoothly flowing current, that we reached the mouth of the McGregor. The Fraser flowed heavily against the north bank there and the embroilment of the two rivers was somewhat treacherous. We decided to put in a few hundred yards upstream, thinking it best to scout the McGregor mouth on foot for our initial campsite. We could see that the river's mouth and the lands immediately to the north were oddly shrouded in mists, or was it smoke? This was itself puzzling, because the weather had been fine for more than a week, and there was no reason yet to expect forest fires—the spring had been a wet one. The mists soon turned out to be sweet-smelling and warm. Angus concluded that their source was the different water temperatures of the two rivers, and I could think of no other explanation.

We beached our craft and hauled it up. I left Angus and young Jimmie, and scouted inland for a campsite. For a week or two, we would be moving up the McGregor, and it was my expectation, on the basis of Mackenzie's word, that the river could be navigated for some distance.

I didn't have far to walk. We'd come ashore at a narrow neck between the two rivers, no more than a hundred yards across. From there, the McGregor veered north, and formed a bulb-like promontory a quarter mile across, treed mainly by poplars in a uniform array and with an absence of underbrush. I found a spot within the lea of the land with gentle current and an upland clear and low enough to let the breezes wafting down the river clear the air a little of the insects. I called the men to bring the boat around, I cleared the spot I'd chosen, and together we made our camp.

The light stays long in the north at that time of the year, and so our camp was complete well before the eleven p.m. dusk. Jimmie had put the fishing lines in the river shortly after we arrived and within the hour we were able to pull out four dolly varden trout, which Angus prepared for our meal. I busied myself with building a large mapping table out of the pitch-free poplars, and over it I secured a stretch of canvas. Then I built a bench to sit on, and had the next day's tasks set down before the natural light gave way. Out on the river, the main bank of the mist seemed to have withdrawn to midstream, leaving our camp dry and airy but thoroughly obscuring the northern bank.

Angus noticed it first. "Have you marked it, August? I've not seen a single mosquito since we made camp."

I looked up from my papers. "You're right," I agreed. "What do you make of it? The breeze isn't strong enough to accomplish that."

"I never question a blessing," he laughed. "Perhaps it's the mist."

"No mist here," Jimmie interjected. He was standing on a log that jutted out into the stream, looking out across the water. "The mist stays in midstream. It hasn't moved since we got here."

I stacked my papers and set the heavy leather mapping case on top of them to guard against the breeze. I'd fully expected the mist to cover the campsite by now, spreading as the air cooled. Instead it undulated in midstream, as if tethered. I walked to the campfire and poured the last of the coffee from the enamel pot into the moss.

"We have a lot to do tomorrow," I said. "Time for some sleep."

It was a new moon, and on an impulse, I slept outside the tent that first night. As I lay in my sleeping bag beneath the sky, watching the milky way, a strange bird began to sing—a stutter at first, as if it found song difficult. But then it broke free into a sweet soaring note that found swift answer—the same stutter, followed by the soaring; deeper, longer, sweeter still. I listened for a few moments, enchanted, before sleep took me. As I drifted off, I felt sure the mist would stay on its side of the river.

•

The next morning we began our survey, leaving the mystery of the mist and the unknown bird for later. We embarked with the roar of the kicker, and steered our way up the McGregor, keeping to the south side of the river outside the mist, which ended no more than a mile upstream, veering off through the forest to nestle at the base of the Monkmans. With the disappearance of the mist the insects returned, and with a vengeance. Small creeks boiled and sputtered into the McGregor here and there, their acidic yellow-green contents quickly lost in the river's murkier water save for the irregular line of foam that streamed across the surface. After a few uneventful miles upstream, we turned into Herrick Creek, and thence to James Creek, the infamous "Bad River" of Mackenzie's voyage to the Pacific. In its upper reaches, their canoe broke up, and much equipment was lost, including the greater part of their shot. Several of the crewmen were almost drowned, including Mackenzie himself, who was swept downstream in an attempt—a successful one—to save the irreplaceable navigational instruments.

Mackenzie, I recall, had come through it at high water, during what must have been a particularly bad year. But his "Bad River", when we saw it, was not all that bad. It was like a thousand other northern creeks, cluttered with debris, passable by boat only in places, bordered alternately by hillside and swamp, bedeviled by insects of all kinds. Yet it was nothing out of the ordinary, and we mapped its length in five days.

We returned to our base camp on the evening of the fifth day and feasted as we had each day on trout, then settled in for an evening of rest. We planned no work the next day, and the fine weather seemed to be holding. But the mist across from us had remained, a little thinner perhaps, but still constant in midstream. Once again I slept outside the tent, delighted at the absence of insects, my senses feasting on the crescent moon and the delightful song of the unknown birds across the river.

The next morning I suggested to the men that we investigate the region behind the mists. Angus quickly agreed, but Jimmie Paquette immediately grew morose. He told us he didn't like the idea of going over there, but would not say why. Angus, mutter-ing something about the superstitious Indians, first turned away, and then irritably suggested that I order him to go. But Jimmie stoutly refused, his face darkening at Angus' taunts, and I didn't force the issue, even though Angus went so far as to suggest that Jimmie might be thinking of lighting out on us while we were gone. But he'd have no boat, since we would use it to cross the river, and I couldn't see him trekking the harsh miles back to town overland and alone.

On an impulse, I took along my survey instruments and the ancient bellows camera I'd inherited from a deceased uncle, and Angus and I pushed off. The opposite bank was invisible because of the mist, and when we reached it, we discovered that a dense thicket of evergreens commenced only a few feet from shore. The trees were of an unfamiliar species, and I took a specimen to iden-tify later, despite Angus' opinion that their strangeness was due to a trick of the light. We moved with some difficulty into the thicket. The mist appeared to be thinning out, and so did the trees, and I discovered to my consternation that shapes appeared to be moving through them on a course parallel with our own.

I heard Angus stop. "Perhaps we shouldn't go any farther," he said, almost stammering. "I don't much like this."

"The way looks easier," I answered, trying to be reassuring but not entirely convinced he was wrong. "Let's see what's up ahead."

Just as I said that, one of the shapes altered its course and moved toward us. I was startled to find that it was a white-tailed deer. It ambled toward me and stopped a few feet away.

"Angus," I said. "Look at this."

"I know," he answered tensely. "We're bloody well surrounded by them."

We were, but that was not the only surprise. They were soon milling around us like a pack of friendly dogs: does, fawns, bucks with still-furry antlers. Nor were they all white-tailed deer. Among them were the slightly larger mule deer, and several very small animals of a species I was not familiar with. One magnificent buck was clearly a European red deer. I glanced at Angus, saw from his eyes that he was close to panic, and took charge as best I could.

"Well, this is a bit odd," I said. "Let's see what happens if we try to move. We can't stand here forever."

I took a step forward, reaching out as I did so to touch one of the animals, a young white-tailed doe. She jerked her head away, not abruptly, to keep out of my reach. I took another step forward, and the animals began to make way for me. I could hear them closing in behind me.

"Come on, Angus," I said. "There doesn't seem to be anything to fear."

Very slowly, we made our way out of the mist, escorted by the deer. The trees disappeared behind us, and we were standing on the edge of a lagoon of perfectly clear, still water. In the deep water, I could see trout darting here and there. A short distance away was a sturdy footbridge, and on the other side was something more astounding: an enormous formal garden, dotted here and there by more deer, and beyond that, a mansion, much like those I'd seen in pictures of the English countryside.

"What in God's name do you make of it?" I asked Angus, and without waiting for his answer, made for the bridge. He said nothing, but his footsteps behind me assured me that he was following.

The deer followed us too, a kind of escort. The great red buck trotted ahead and stood by the bridge, as if inviting us to cross it. We did so, our heavy caulked boots echoing loudly on the thick planks, and started along a wide path paved with large flat stones.

Angus broke his silence to comment on the fine workmanship of the paving. He was from a family of stonemasons and had briefly worked the trade himself in Scotland before emigrating.

Naturally it was the gardens that interested me. Everything I could see was exotic in origin. A huge spreading white oak dominated the central part of the garden, and closer to the mansion stood an enormous plane tree, its broad branches reaching out and up to make it the perfect image of what a tree should be. The pathway was bordered by fruit trees: apples, cherries, plums, each laden with young fruit. No two trees were alike, and many of them species I couldn't identify. The flower beds were likewise filled with exotica. There were roses, salpiglosis, cascading petunias and geraniums, gentians, and edging the pathway, a flood of electric blue lobelia. There was a preponderance of white roses, the most fragile shade of all, and impossible to grow within 400 miles of this region. Indeed, if there was any logic to the garden, it lay in its uniform impossibility. Few, if any, of these plants would normally thrive in this harsh environment. The pattern of the blossomings was similar—most of them were out of season. Yet it was too dazzling for disbelief, like the deer had been, and I willingly let all of it in. Preposterously, I had blundered into paradise, into what seemed to be the Garden of Eden itself. I turned to glance at Angus, and his expression, no longer fearful, echoed my own emotions.

The great stag still cantered along in front of us, leading the way, and before it loomed the mansion. Was there a mansion in the Garden of Eden? If so, it had been there a long time. The great structure, built entirely of stone, was aged and weathered by the elements. Along one entire wall boston ivy coursed across the stones, partially masking several gargoyles that jutted from the roof and cornices. Like the grounds, the building seemed well kept but not manicured, although several of the window casements, Angus noted, were in need of repair. Despite its impossibility, the mansion and its grounds were overwhelmingly, materially, real. And as we stood, looking around with a mixture of scientific curiosity and awe, a voice confirmed our impressions.

"It's quite real, gentleman. There are no illusions here but your own."

99

I spun around and saw a woman standing on the porch not more than a dozen feet from us, stroking the forehead of the stag. I was struck dumb for a moment, and merely stood gawking. She appeared to be about my age, fair-haired, her body simply clothed in a pale grey smock. A set of keys hung from a linen belt around her waist. She was not beautiful: her features were regular, but exuded a severity that instantly precluded sensuality, and there was an almost businesslike candour in her gaze that dampened terror and attraction alike.

"Having come this far," she continued when we remained speechless, "would you like to see the house?"

I choked out an affirmative answer, and she turned and strode briskly through the doors, leaving them open for us to follow.

"My God," I heard Angus say. "Have you ever seen such beauty?"

"It is magnificent," I replied. "We should go in."

"No, no. Not *it*. Her."

Still wondering what he meant, I entered the mansion.

•

I have not seen a building to match its grandeur to this day. The entrance hall was as large in area as the house I'd grown up in, and panelled to the ceiling with age-darkened oak. We followed the blond woman from room to magnificent room without speaking. She seemed content to let us dwell within our own thoughts, and I was glad of that. It was more than enough of a mental effort to take all of it in. I was incapable of interpreting its meaning, or of formulating the questions that enable comprehension. Meaning and questions would have to come later.

We came to another panelled room, this one apparently the library. There were bookcases filled with volume after leather-bound volume, up to the twelve-foot ceilings. In the centre of the room was a great oak table. The woman pulled up a chair at its far end and sat down, motioning us to do likewise.

"I've shown you but a small part of the house," she said briskly. "And now I have some duties of my own to take care of. Please

100

feel free to roam at will. If you have questions, I will answer them at lunch.''

"Where will I find you?" Angus said, emphasizing the singular 'I' in an odd way.

"I will find you," she laughed. "Don't worry about such matters.''

For reasons I could not isolate, I found the woman rather unpleasant to look at. But Angus could not take his eyes off her. She got up from the table, put the chair back in its place, smiled and left the room. I watched Angus follow her with his eyes. When she closed the door behind her, he continued to stare.

"Angus," I said.

He tore his attention from the door, and met my eyes reluctantly. "I'm fine," he said, answering my unasked question. "I'd like to look around.''

"Let's look together," I suggested.

"No," he answered firmly. "Alone.''

I agreed to respect his need for solitude with some misgiving, and we ambled off in different directions. My first task was to satisfy my surveyor's curiosity. Since they obviously existed in exception to the landscape and climate, the mansion and its grounds must have limits and boundaries. I set out to locate them.

It took me less than an hour to establish them. I was on an island, probably a natural one created long ago by an oxbow in the McGregor River. The island was perhaps a mile across and slightly less than two miles long. The water in the moat was perfectly still but without a trace of stagnancy, as if renewed from an unseen spring. There seemed to be no intermixture with the much murkier and colder McGregor. The mansion was the lone building on the island, and it was T-shaped, 278 feet along the front, wings fifty-eight feet in depth, and of an architectural style I was able to date, very roughly, in the early nineteenth century. At the far end of the island was a strange structure—not a building—but a large enclosure exactly 200 feet along each side, and walled with large stones quite unlike those of the mansion. At the midpoint of the south wall was an enormous solid gate, which was locked with a huge padlock. I could not see what was inside the enclosure because of the height of the walls.

From there I returned to the garden to reconnoitre, and was thoroughly engrossed in identifying and listing what plants I could, and making notes on those I couldn't, when I heard a snuffling sound from behind me. It was the stag. As I turned, it turned, walked a few steps toward the mansion, then stopped and looked along its flank, clearly signalling that I was to follow. It allowed me to walk beside it, and I returned to the mansion at a leisurely pace, pleased that it was allowing me to touch it.

Angus was engrossed in conversation with the woman, leaning across the table toward her. She looked up as I entered, and motioned for me to sit at her left, across from Angus.

"Did you have a productive morning, Mr. Jensen?" she asked. I hadn't given her my name, and was startled until I realized that Angus must have told her.

"There is much here to interest a man," I replied formally.

Her laugh spilled out through the room, and its echo sounded oddly bitter. "There is nothing here men haven't seen before," she said as the laughter subsided. "But I am gratified by your scientific interest. A Linnaeus is always welcome."

"I have a thousand questions," I said, taking her comment as an invitation.

"They will have to wait," she said, getting up from the table. "Let me satisfy your bodily hungers first."

She soon returned with a platter of cold venison, another of exquisitely prepared vegetables I was not familiar with, and a mildew-topped bottle of red wine. It was a claret, she explained later, light-bodied and delicate beyond the rough experience of my palate. We ate in silence, despite my bubbling curiosity, and I contented myself by savouring the wine and the subtle flavours of the unknown vegetables. I did not want to offend her, and she carried her silence like a suit of armour. From time to time, however, I saw Angus gazing at her with a mixture of lust and adoration, and his expression troubled me. Finally I could restrain my questions no longer.

"How is it," I said as carefully as I knew how, "that you have come to be here?"

She laughed again, this time without bitterness. "That," she replied after a moment's thought, "will take a very long time to

102

explain. Perhaps you will understand, perhaps not. But right now you could not understand if I told you. Try to satisfy your more immediate curiosities for the time being. I will come and find you later in the day, and we can talk then.''

Angus stood up. Through the meal he had not spoken a word.

"Come," she said, motioning him to follow. It was clear that I was not welcome to join them.

•

Through the afternoon I pursued my interests and was able to establish only one thing as a certainty: nothing I could see was native, except some of the deer. I busied myself with the camera, taking photographs of as many of the island's wonders as I had film for. By midafternoon, my focus shifted from botany to ornithology. I heard the song of the mysterious bird that days ago had filled the night air of the camp, and followed it to a thicket of brilliant crimson blossoms—quince, I think. In it were a pair of dull olive-coloured birds about the size of robins and with a spot of rusty red low on the breast. They were nesting there, and as the afternoon advanced, their song commenced. I observed them for a while, wondering how so sweet a song could come from such an unassuming bird. I also noted several tiny English robins, half the size of the native variety, and a small flock of starlings.

More startling still, I saw, across the moat at regular intervals, falcons, set motionless like sentinels atop the thickets that surrounded the island. And as I watched, one of them rose sharply into the air to strike down a whiskeyjack that swooped toward the gardens. The falcon pinned it to the ground until it ceased to struggle, then carried the broken corpse back to its perch.

I felt sick to my stomach without knowing why. I closed my notebook and began to wander aimlessly through the gardens, past the spreading plane tree, and found myself at the locked gate of the enclosure behind the mansion. I had no notion of the time, except that the sun was rapidly dropping toward the horizon. I felt no hunger, and my curiosity was sated. Dully, I tested the lock on the gate. At my touch, the lock dropped open. I pushed against the heavy doors, they parted, and I slipped inside.

In a symmetrical pattern within the huge enclosure were nine marble statues of classical style, the figures roughly a third larger than life. All were of women, all deeply scarred by the elements. Almost as astounding, and in brutal contrast, was their surrounding landscape. There were trees, the majority leafless and dead, all twisted and distorted by disease and decay. More astonishing yet were the carcasses of deer in varying states of decomposition, some mere skeletons, others recently dead and bloated with maggots. Several deer in the compound were still alive, but barely so. As I watched, an ancient buck tottered toward a statue, gave forth a short bellow of pain, and crumpled at the base.

The day seemed to be darkening rapidly, and the air suddenly filled with a cacophony of birdsong. A dying tree close to the nearest statue was covered with the olive-coloured birds I'd seen earlier, but here their warblings were neither sweet nor clear. The song stuttered to life, as before, but then it wavered and died stillborn. I gathered myself for a closer examination of the statues. Then I remember nothing.

•

I was awakened in the mansion by Jimmie Paquette. As I soon discovered, more than a day had passed. Jimmie had found me sleeping on the grounds, and, unable to rouse me, had carried me into the house. He seemed anxious about my well-being, but not overly troubled by his surroundings.

"Where's Angus?" he said.

I struggled to my feet. "I don't know," I said, still disoriented. "Haven't you seen him?"

"Not here," he said flatly.

"He's got to be here. Have you seen the woman?"

"What woman? I haven't seen nobody around here except you and a few deer. Strange place."

"I'm afraid your Mr. MacKay has made himself a trifle ill," said a female voice behind us. "Could you give me a hand bringing him in?"

Jimmie gave the woman a strange look, and followed her out

104

the door. I felt disoriented, and I sat down in the nearest chair while the two of them carried Angus into the room and laid him out flat on the floor. He was unconscious.

"What's happened to him?" I demanded.

"See for yourself. He's drunk himself into a stupor." There was an iciness in her voice that betrayed her contempt. "He'll have to sleep it through."

I demanded to know how it had happened, but she merely shrugged. And before I could ask her further questions, she turned on her heel and left the room, closing the door behind her as if to make sure we didn't follow.

"What do you want to do now?" Jimmie asked.

"I don't know. We may have to wait until Angus is sober enough to move on his own. I don't know how we'll get him through the thicket."

Jimmie waited for me to continue, and his silence brought me to an awareness, for the first time, that I had no idea how he'd gotten there.

"How did you get across the river?" I asked. "There was no boat."

"When you didn't come back last night I got worried that something happened. So I made a raft, upstream a way, and poled it across the river. It took me most of the day. When I run across the bears I get a little scared, but they pay me no mind, like the deer. This is a crazy place."

"Bears?"

"Yeah, I counted nine of them. Grizzlies. But not too big ones. When I fired the gun in the air they took off."

"You've got the gun with you?" He pointed to my 30-30, which was leaning against the wall. For a moment, I felt comforted.

"Did you fire at any of them?"

"Hell, no," he said. "What would I do that for?"

"Did you bring any food with you?"

"I got a thermos of tea in my pack. Maybe we can use it to get Mister MacKay moving."

We tried to, but Angus was truly unconscious, his pupils pin-pricks, and his breath coming in short, shallow gasps. We gave up trying to bring him around, and I sat back heavily against one of the panelled walls. I was still a trifle fuzzy myself. Jimmie, as usual, didn't have much to say. He said that he wanted to get out of there, and the sooner the better, and our conversation kept coming back to that.

Despite the fact that I'd been unconscious for twenty-four hours, I soon found that I was craving sleep. I tried to fight it, but couldn't. I told Jimmie to wake me if the woman returned, lay my head down on the thick carpet and fell asleep almost instantly.

I awoke in the middle of the night. Through the window, the brilliant light of a full moon shone down around me. I experienced a moment of sheer terror—the full moon was still nearly a week away. Then I heard Angus groan in his sleep, and turned to him. His breathing was now regular and deep, and I counted that a blessing. He would, I decided, be fine in the morning, except for the hangover. But Jimmie was nowhere to be seen. A second wave of terror passed through me when I saw that the rifle was gone as well.

For a few moments I sat there in the pool of moonlight, uncertain of what I should do. I didn't want to return to the enclosure, but something told me that Jimmie had gone there, and that I had to get him out. He was my responsibility, even though it had been he who had rescued me from my own brush with whatever was out there in the enclosure. I struggled to my feet, feeling much older than my thirty years, stretched my aching muscles, and made my way cautiously outdoors.

The carpet of moonlight on the lawns was so brilliant that it seemed almost like snow. Here and there I could see the darker shapes of the deer, most of them sleeping beneath the boughs of the trees. One or two browsed on the low branches. To my relief, I could see none of Jimmie's bears.

A short walk brought me to the doors of the enclosure, but before I had to open them, they opened from within and out slipped Jimmie. I whispered his name and he wheeled the gun around and for an instant, I thought he might fire. Then he recognized me, and I saw him relax.

"You're awake," he said, simply.

"The moonlight woke me. What are you doing out here?"

"Nothing." He shrugged. "I woke up and both of you were sleeping, so I went outside. I decided to look around."

"What did you find in there?"

"Nothing much," he said neutrally. "There's nothing in there to see. We should go back to the house before Angus wakes up."

Something in his eyes told me to let it go at that, and I followed him back to the house. On the way, the big buck intercepted us, moving crosswise to us until he blocked Jimmie's path. I thought he might shoot the animal, but he didn't. He merely stroked its back and spoke to it, so quietly I couldn't make out the words. The buck moved on and let us pass, then brought up the rear.

Angus was still sleeping, but I told Jimmie we could wake him if we wanted. He agreed that we should. I leaned down and shook his shoulder hard, and he rolled over. I could see panic in his face as he fought his way to consciousness. He opened his eyes.

"August," he said hoarsely. "Good lord, it's you. Where are they?"

"They?" I swear I saw his mind close behind the open eyes. He rolled onto his side, away from us.

"Mister MacKay," Jimmie said, moving forward to grasp his shoulder. "We're going to go now. How are you feeling?"

Angus rolled over to face us. "Paquette?"

"It's me, yeah."

Angus relaxed. "I can't leave here yet. I've got to stay on."

"We go *now*," Jimmie said, firmly.

"He's right, Angus," I said. "This isn't a safe place."

"I seen a lot of bears," Jimmie added.

Angus began to laugh, first to himself, and then at us, but there was no mirth in his laughter. "I don't want to leave this place. I've got no reason to leave."

"This isn't a place," I said. "I don't know what it is. But it isn't any place we can stay in safely."

Jimmie grunted. "Let's stop talking and get the hell out of here."

•

I found the camera and the survey equipment, and allowed

107

Jimmie to lead us back to the boat. We didn't have to hogtie MacKay to get him to leave, but we had to threaten to. I'd have almost preferred it if we'd had to. When he agreed to leave with us, something in him broke, and the life went out of him.

•

We did finish the survey. After another week I moved our camp farther up the river, away from those mists that still hovered in midstream. By an unspoken agreement, we didn't talk about the island. Angus didn't talk about anything after that if he could avoid it. He did his job well enough, but as I said, it was as if the spark had gone out of him, and it didn't come back.

When we got back to town at the end of August, MacKay collected his pay and disappeared without a word. I sent the film off to be developed that first day, and when it came back I thought the film-processing company had gotten my film mixed up with someone else's. The pictures were of an island, but all that was on it was some marsh grass and thickets of young poplar and willows. But when I looked closer I saw the mist in the background of several photos, and I knew they were mine.

I never got the chance to speak with Angus MacKay again. Two months after he disappeared they fished him out of the river south of town. The town coroner was an old friend of mine and I spoke to him several days after the inquest. He questioned me about Angus, wanting to know if anything had happened up on the survey.

I'd already spoken to Jimmie about keeping quiet about what we'd seen, so I couldn't very well talk about it myself. I told the coroner that it'd been more or less routine, and asked why he was asking. He said that the night we got back Angus had gone down to the bar and gotten drunk, and that he'd been saying some strange things.

"Angus always said strange things when he had money enough to get drunk," I said.

"This was different. He said he couldn't live any more, that he had to go back up to some island. And you know that Angus was always a pretty heavy-set fellow?"

108

"That's true," I admitted.

"Well," the coroner said, shaking his head, "When I examined the body there were some strange things about it. He'd not been in the water more than a day or so, so the body wasn't too far gone. I'm not sure that he drowned at all."

"How did he die if he didn't drown? Surely he wasn't murdered?"

"Nothing like that. I think he might have starved to death."

•

So that's my story. Sure to God, I never went back there again. The only other thing to add is that about two weeks ago I had a visit from Jimmie Paquette. He's close to seventy now, and he left the area not long after we came back from that island. Went off to live back east, I think. He came back about five years ago, fairly well-to-do, and in good health. He'd remained a bachelor, like I had. I spoke to him several times, but there wasn't much to talk about. But I guess he found out I was about to pass on, and came to visit me.

After a few minutes of awkwardness, he broached the subject of the trip up the river, so I asked him some questions about what he'd seen.

"It was a strange place," he recalled, settling in his chair as if we were finally about to get down to business. "I remember the mist, and the deer, and the bears of course. But what I couldn't make sense of at the time was what Angus kept saying about not leaving, and about the women."

"Women?" I echoed. "There was only one woman. He never said anything about there being more than one."

"He said something to me one day when you were out checking a line. It was the only time. He told me there were eight or nine more of them, the most beautiful women he'd ever come across, and lascivious—yeah, that's the word he used, and I remember it because I had to ask him what it meant—beyond imagination. Those were his words: 'lascivious beyond imagination.' Then he clammed up again, tight as a drum. What I want to know is if you knew about them."

109

"I saw some statues of women in the walled enclosure behind the mansion, that's all."

Jimmie's head snapped up. "You saw statues in that pen? All I saw was a hovel, and the old woman who lived there."

"What old woman?" I asked, startled. "You mean the woman who lived in the house? She was about my age, grey dress, and if I recall it correctly, she carried some big keys in a chain around her waist."

"The crone carried keys and wore a grey dress. But she wasn't young. She must have been in her eighties."

"That night, Jimmie. You left while I was sleeping and went to the enclosure."

"I woke up and saw her standing at the door. She motioned me to come, so I did. I picked up the rifle first, then I followed her outside. She walked to the pen. I wanted to ask her what was going on, and why she was living there. She wouldn't tell me anything—she talked, but it was mostly in some foreign language. I got angry with her, but all she would say is that if I didn't get you and Angus out of there, the place would kill you both." He looked up. "So I got you out of there. The place was making both of you see things."

"It was a magnificent place," I said. "I still wonder how that building came to be there, and the gardens."

"Wasn't so great," he said, frowning. "A couple of shacks in a poplar glade. Maybe a few grizzlies and some deer, but that's all. And a crazy old lady who could make you guys see things."

Weasels

In the years just before the world became a global village, life was hard, and it was very unorganized. There weren't television programs to show people what life is like in Los Angeles, and so nobody knew what was really going on. People couldn't watch their television sets because there weren't any, and they couldn't go down to the shopping centres to buy all those brand name products they'd seen on television because there weren't any shopping centres. There really wasn't much to do in those olden days, so people spent their time working hard, and playing at games they had to make up all by themselves. Up in the north, it was a long way to the big city, and the government left everybody alone to play whatever games they wanted to, and to invent new games whenever they were needed.

Getting drunk was the game that consumed most of the people who lived in the smaller towns, at least those people who weren't just there to work real hard and save their money so they could get the hell out of there and live in the big city near shopping centres, and where the government had everything figured out for you. Those people weren't interested in having fun. They were only interested in going to church or to the bank, and in how to walk around with a long face in a snowstorm without having icicles hanging out of their noses. They had only one game, and that consisted of trying to talk entirely in business slogans, and a few of them were pretty damned good at it too. But to most northerners, that didn't seem like much fun, because they still believed that when you said something, you were supposed to know what it meant.

Like any other game, getting drunk had its rules. The rules the northerners made up for the game were so effective they haven't changed much over the years, except that some of the old enthusiasm has faded. Nowadays a lot of people just sit in front of a television set in their trailers and drink privately until they fall asleep. That isn't much of a game, so I'll tell you the rules to the old public game, which were as follows:
(1)   Sit down
(2)   Drink beer
(3)   Drink more beer
(4)   Drink even more beer
(5)   Stand up
(6)   Try to walk to the washroom
(7)   Pee (a really skilled player will fall into the urinal during this part of the game)
(8)   Find your table again
(9)   Sit down without knocking over the table
(10) Drink beer
(11) Drink more beer
(12) Drink even more beer
(13) Stand up
(14) Pass out.

There were some game options, of course. The most common were that anywhere after rule (3) above one could:
(i)   Argue loudly and irrationally
(ii)   Fight.

Another frequently exercised option could occur anywhere after rule (5). It had two parts:
(i)   Turn green

112

(ii)   Vomit (special bonus points awarded for projectile vomiting).

Getting drunk could be, and was, played in a wide variety of situations, and without regard for race, colour or creed. All that was required was money, a body, and, of course, a willingness to lose the money and to suffer the hangovers. As games go it was relatively simple, and intensely democratic. There were a few exotic denouements, naturally. Favourites were Homicidal Driving of Motor Vehicles, Abuse of Loved Ones, Sexual Harassment of Strangers, Sexual Incompetence, and Going Out After Closing Time to Eat Chinese Food.

And there were traditions. The most important of these was to speak the following phrase as loudly as possible at the beginning of each game: "Whoopie! Let's go bite the heads off some weasels!" This phrase was always followed by a refrain, as follows: "Whoopie! Great idea! We'll suck on a few darts while we're at it!"

•

"Whoopie!" was the sole political slogan used in the north, and as those who understand the nature of the global village know very well, slogans are the only truly important content of human language. But for the northerners, who believed that slogans are really just a sign of altered or reduced consciousness, this slogan, and the traditional game ritual it initiated, only got them into trouble. The roads were getting better, and with them so were what the government men called communications and progress. What this meant was that the government was sending more and more of its representatives up north to figure out what it had to do to keep on getting elected. One afternoon, just as some folks were beginning The Game, they were overheard by an agent from the government.

The government agent decided that something was very wrong, and set a report back to the government saying that the northerners were engaged in unsavoury practices. Soon the town was swarming with government agents in suits and uniforms who said that they were there to put a stop to the mistreatment of poor fur-bearing animals and other abuses.

For several weeks the agents combed the town looking for the kennels where the weasels were being kept prior to ritual slaughter. Eventually someone suggested that if they went down to a bar they could bite the heads off a few for themselves. To a man, the agents all shouted "Ahah!" (a common government slogan still in wide use) and stormed into the nearest bar to rescue the poor animals.

It wasn't very long before they discovered just what a weasel was, and the agents went back to the big city, red-faced but wiser in the ways of the north.

That wasn't the end of it. A short time later yet another wave of government agents descended on the town and held some meetings at the high school. They sat up on the stage and talked to the bank managers' wives and a few schoolteachers about how there wasn't enough of what they called "culture" in the north, and how the people needed better things to do than to sit around getting drunk and sucking on, and no doubt occasionally swallowing, dangerously pointed objects.

Not even the bank managers' wives and the schoolteachers knew what they were talking about this time. But the government agents didn't notice. They buzzed amongst themselves and nodded their heads to indicate to their dumbfounded audience that yes indeed, *they* knew what they were talking about, and that they knew exactly what was on the minds of everyone in the audience.

Since this kind of behaviour was nothing new to their audience, everybody let the government men go on talking to one another up on the stage until they'd decided amongst themselves that they had it all figured out. Then the government men all had dinner with the Rotary Club and went back to the big city without ever coming down to the bars to get drunk with the people they said they were there to help out.

•

A few months later the government passed a law that said that from here on in there was a game called darts that people all across the north must play while getting drunk, adding that the new

114

law provided a humane method of preventing folks from eating darts and making themselves vomit.

The northerners thought the new law was pretty odd, but then they thought that most of the things the government did were odd. They knew how to play darts, but they thought it wasn't the sort of game you should play while you were getting drunk. The owners of the bars didn't like it at all, and they sent a telegram to the government saying that the new law wasn't a very good idea and that it was better for folks to punch one another or throw beer glasses while they were getting drunk, just like they always had.

But the government replied that playing darts would make the northerners more cultured and happier. Better than eating them, they added in private, and went on to vote themselves a raise for their good works.

•

It wasn't very long before the inevitable happened. Two very big and very drunk loggers just out of logging camp foolishly began a game of darts. One of them knocked over his opponent's beer glass, and the affronted logger naturally threw the table at his clumsy co-player. Everyone in the bar remained seated and continued to drink, because this was a thoroughly normal event most of them had seen a hundred times before. But the clumsy logger happened to have a government dart in his hand, and, as he dodged the flying table, he quite naturally threw it at his co-player.

The dart selected an old man who had been drunk for most of the last twenty years, and lodged itself smack in the side of his head. He looked startled for just a second before he became a very dead old man with a dart sticking out of his head. Then he collapsed onto the table in front of him, sending a whole nest of weasels flying.

Within a week there were enough dart-related incidents to fill a large dossier, some, as you can imagine, at least as gruesome as the one described. The reports of the incidents piled up on a desk somewhere in the government offices in the big city, until eventually the government sent a special investigator to find out why all of a sudden so many people were having difficulty with the government's enlightened cultural program. He was quite an intelligent man, this investigator, since the first thing he did when he got to town was to go to the first bar he found and sit down with some folks who were biting the heads off some weasels and ducking the government darts that were flying all around the room.

"How do you like it?" asked one of the drinkers, who'd pretty much adjusted to the government darts and didn't think there was anything special about them.

"How do I like what?" replied the special investigator from underneath the table. The northerners thought he looked pretty funny crouching under the table, and they laughed. One of them offered him a cigarette, sticking the pack right under the special investigator's nose.

"Care for a dart?" he asked.

Greenie

Benson pushed his knapsack farther under the helicopter seat and gazed out at the unbroken carpet of forest beneath the bubble. It doesn't matter that you're afraid, he told himself. What matters is that this is an adventure. Real Life. You live in the north, you're a northerner, and now you're really seeing what it means.

He glanced across at Ratson, the pilot. Ratson caught his eye and raised his thumb in a gesture Benson recognized but didn't understand.

"What is it?" Benson yelled, leaning toward the other man to penetrate the din from the rotors.

A grin broke across Ratson's handsome face and he waved Benson's question away without answering it, settling instead into a rhetorical check of his equipment: look at the instrumentation, look up at the rotor spinning overhead, look down at the trees, tap the stick with his right hand, shrug and resettle. He was flying with a greenhorn, and the equipment check was designed more to impress than anything else.

•

It was May 1963. Benson was a passenger in a helicopter hired by the Forest Service, headed for a camp on the Findlay River, about 150 miles northeast of Prince George. A few days before, he'd hired on as a Forest Service compassman. His government-issue knapsack was full of new gear, most of it issued by the Service, and the rest, raingear, boots, etc., bought on the advice of the kindly ranger who'd phoned to tell him he had the job.

He would be working, said the ranger, with one of the crews currently cruising the 600 square miles that would end up under water as a result of the Peace River dam, the latest and grandest of a series of government hydroelectric projects. That's all Benson knew about it; he wasn't even sure what cruising was, except that cruisers were men who went into the wildest areas, made detailed surveys of the terrain and estimated how much timber was there so the loggers could cut it down. At the Forest Service office in Prince George he'd gone to the trouble of asking what it was that he would be doing if they hired him. The man who had taken his application frowned, and said that he'd find out what he needed to know when he got the job, if he got it at all. And his frown made that seem unlikely.

But he'd gotten the job after all. And now he was almost there, and he still didn't know what he was going to be doing. He would have to choose between his curiosity and his fear of appearing to be a greenhorn, and it wasn't a choice he looked forward to. Smart people, he'd learned, hid their ignorance, and he didn't want to appear any more stupid than he was. His ignorance, it seemed to him, had always been greater than that of the people around him.

In the distance he saw a series of small clearings in the trees. "What's that down there?" he yelled to Ratson.

"That's where you're going, Greenie," Ratson answered, then nodded his head in the direction of the tangled ribbon of water to the west. "That's one of the rivers they're going to put under 500 feet of water."

"Is that right?" Benson answered, not loud enough to expect a response. He'd heard a little about the dam the government

118

planned, but it hadn't meant much to him until now. The countryside, now that he was close enough to examine it, was rugged and foreign. Dotting the forest, which undulated in height and colour as the terrain shifted or the species of timber changed, were frequent open patches. Swamps, he thought. He'd been warned about them. The bugs were supposed to be worse here, and there was a lot of devil's club, whatever that was. He had no basis for comparison; bush was bush, and until now he'd stayed out of it.

Benson was a city boy. He'd done some canoeing and camping like everyone did, and he'd swum in the lakes, in spite of the bloodsuckers. But his father worked in the city, and he'd had little contact with the lumbering industry he was told powered the economy of the town. He'd listened to the night whine of the planer mills since he was a small child, fallen under the pall of ash pumped out by the slash burners, and seen the logging trucks come and go with their loads of newly cut logs or milled planks. Such things were a natural part of his environment, like the rivers and the trees. Big deal. As a child he'd been interested in more immediate things, mostly of his own imagining, and as a teenager, cars and girls had been his preoccupation.

That he'd stayed in high school as long as he had indicated that he wasn't headed in the direction of the mills. For that, you quit school early, spent your winters and summers in the bush, and in the spring and fall you bought a car and drove it around the streets, waiting for the mills to reopen. You got into fights and drank a lot of beer, and if you were unlucky you felled a tree on yourself, or a snapped choker-cable took your head off. Or if that didn't happen, you got married and lived in a trailer, and your kids ran around among the other trailers in the camps, your wife got fat, and you worked on your car and drank when you weren't working in the bush.

Benson wasn't sure what he wanted out of life, but he did know he didn't want any of those things. So, when he couldn't see much of anything else coming his way, he'd joined the Forest Service.

Ratson's voice snapped him out of his reverie. "Going down. Hold on."

Beneath his feet at the far edge of a swamp, Benson could see the clearing the helicopter was headed for. A green 4x4 travelall van was parked at its edge, headlights on.

"That's your pickup," Ratson yelled. "Already waiting."

They floated down near the edge of the clearing and Ratson dropped the sling of supplies they'd been carrying beneath the craft. Then he moved it toward centre of the clearing, alighted, and Ratson clicked off a series of switches that sent the engine of the helicopter into a rapidly sagging chup.

"Climb out," Ratson ordered. "Watch out for the rotors."

Benson scrambled out as two men clambered off the travelall's hood and moved uncertainly toward the aircraft. But as he did, his foot caught on the doorsill, and he spilled out onto the soggy ground. One of the men rolled his eyes in a eloquent gesture of mock despair, the other laughed.

"New boots," Benson explained sheepishly.

"New everything, from the look of it," said the eye-roller. He was an older man, heavy-set, in his 30s. The laugher was about Benson's age, and part Indian. Behind Benson, Ratson began to unload the helicopter, throwing Benson's new gear into the mud first, then tossing boxes of supplies on top of it.

"Eggs!" the older man shouted, rushing to stop Ratson. "There's supposed to be eggs in there."

"Relax," replied Ratson. "They're here. In the back." He lifted out a carton marked eggs and handed it to him.

"I'll get the stuff in the sling," offered the native. Benson followed him and together they loaded the supplies into the truck. Neither of his co-workers introduced himself, and Benson didn't stop to ask for names.

"I've got another load to come from Hudson Hope," said Ratson when the helicopter was clear of its load. "It'll take about two hours, but I'm dropping it at Camp Two. Radio up and tell them to be waiting, will you?"

The older man nodded, waved his hand in Ratson's direction, and the three of them watched Ratson climb back into the helicopter seat and start the engine.

As the helicopter lifted off, the older man turned to Benson and offered his hand.

"You're Benson, I guess," he said. "I'm Al Mackay. This here is Ray Cardinal."

120

Benson extended his hand for the formality, but Cardinal didn't shake it. "How're you doing, Greenie," he said amiably. "You ever spent any time in the bush?"

"A little," Benson answered. "But not like this. Not working."

"Where you from?" Mackay asked.

"Prince George," Benson said, feeling a small confidence in that. "Born there."

"Well," the older man said, "that's something. Most of the greenies they've been sending us lately come from the coast."

"Oh?" Benson didn't quite know what that meant or if he was supposed to respond.

"Yeah," Cardinal interrupted. "The bugs eat coast greenies. They all want to go home to mommie after a week. Most of them do. When they quit we feed them to the grizzlies."

Benson laughed. Cardinal looked at him hard for a moment, then laughed too. "You'll be okay," Cardinal said. "You've got a few smarts, maybe."

•

It took about a month, but gradually Benson began to understand that he was, as a matter of fact, okay. For the first two weeks, the bugs drove him crazy, getting underneath his gear and even between his glasses and his eyes. He went through bottle after bottle of repellent until he learned to stop eating bananas and stopped washing himself.

He enjoyed the work, his own job as lead compassman, and he liked being outdoors. Cruising, it turned out, was interesting, a series of geometric rituals. Every ten chains, or, as he learned, every 660 feet, the crew stopped, measured a plot of timber, took the diameters and species of each tree within the plot and drilled several of the dominant species to determine their age. After the day was over, they translated the information collected in the field into statistical estimates of the timber available, its quality and age. He was quick and accurate with the numbers, and Mackay taught him the rudiments of map-making. In the bush he learned to move through the always-wet underbrush without getting his hands quilled with devil's club spines, and he easily mastered the

121

techniques of compassing straight lines and of handling the small axes with which they blazed the lines that would later allow the loggers to read the cruising maps.

He had little in common with either of his working mates, but he was, for Mackay, a quick and interested student, and for Cardinal, a cheerful victim for the usual greenhorn practical jokes. Mackay had spent most of his life in the north country, preferring cruising to the more lucrative but noisy and dangerous work of logging. Benson could find out little else about him. Cardinal didn't know where he went for breakup and freezeup, and told Benson that he shouldn't ask stupid questions. Mackay made it clear in his own way that he didn't like talking about his personal life, although he seemed curious enough about everyone else around him.

At first Benson was a little afraid of Cardinal. He came from a well-known Métis family, many of whom were famous for mayhem of one sort or another. More than one of the Cardinals had spent time in jail, and Ray intimated that he was among that group. But he liked to play cards, and because Mackay didn't, Benson soon became his partner at gin rummy. Mackay preferred to spend his free time fishing in the river, or reading. He read adventure magazines, and Western novels, mainly Louis L'Amour and Zane Grey, sometimes reading one novel over two or three times in succession.

There were two other crews in their camp, and at any given week eight or nine men. Each crew had its own tent and cooking arrangements, and the crews, Benson found, tended to stick to themselves, although practical jokes between one crew and another were daily occurrences.

Since it was near flood time, the river was high, and the roads into the camp, bad at the best of times, were impassable. The supplies came in by helicopter every three or four days: steak, eggs, fresh fruit and vegetables. Once, though, a riverboat brought in a big load of staples. The riverboaters were strange, older men, silent and angry. Mackay told Benson that the dam would end their trade forever, and a few of them had spent their whole lives on the river. They didn't like the Forest Service or their helicopters much, he said. The only reason the government was using them at all any more, according to Mackay, was they were buying them off this way. As long as they still had work, they wouldn't make much of a stink about what was going to happen in the future. And for them, said Mackay bleakly, there wasn't a future.

•

About the middle of June, a ranger flew into camp with Ratson and called the crews together. There was a big change being made, he said, looking very pleased with himself. The government had decided that conventional cruising was too slow. It wasn't the fault of the crews, he assured them. They were all doing a great job. It was just that the government was in a hurry. The crews were to finish cruising the dam basin, as he called it, by helicopter. Two helicopters would be stationed there for the rest of the summer, and each pilot would be assigned a two-man crew. Plot-taking would be reduced, mainly to those spots where the helicopters could land easily, and only minimal perimeter surveying would be required.

Benson looked around to see how the others were taking this news. Cardinal and the others were pleased, but Mackay was frowning. Benson wondered what was bothering him, but then he too got caught up in the prospect of spending his days sitting in a helicopter, and forgot about it.

He listened to the ranger explain the new method without really understanding how it was supposed to work. That didn't bother him—Mackay would understand, and he'd explain later. But it did mean that the crews would be reorganized, and that he'd probably end up working with someone else.

Back in the tent that evening Mackay explained the new system. There wasn't that much to explain, but, Benson decided, something about it bothered Mackay. Ground crews would set markers that would be visible from the air, either by falling trees or by hanging long streamers of plastic ribbon in the branches. The air crews would then use these as locational survey points, and would make passes back and forth to estimate tree heights, size and species, and to map the general topographic features. To Benson, it sounded easy, and fun.

"Who am I going to be working with?" he asked.

"With me for the first few days," Mackay said. "Ray can run the ground crew. He doesn't like flying. I'll teach you how to do the surveying, and then I'm going on the ground crew, sort of."

"Why walk when you can fly?" Benson said.

Mackay's face flashed with sudden anger. He seemed on the verge of saying something, then decided against it, turned, and flung his steel survey sheet cover into the corner of the tent. He left the tent, but Benson didn't follow him. Cardinal, who was lying on his cot reading an old issue of *Playboy* Ratson had given him, had nothing to add, except that he'd never seen Mackay act like that.

"Maybe he thinks this isn't real cruising," he offered. "And maybe it isn't. He'll get over it."

•

It was several days before the working helicopters flew in to begin the aerial cruising, and a couple of days more before Benson found out what was sticking in Mackay's craw.

Cruising by helicopter was, as predicted, easy and fast. In four hours they were able to cruise an area that would have taken a week by the old method, even though Mackay insisted that the pilot drop them to take plots at every spot that enabled a landing. When they returned to camp, Mackay swung out of the helicopter seat before the aircraft was firmly down. Benson scrambled after him, and when they were out of the clearing, Mackay turned to him.

"Now I'll show you how to cook this stew," he said.

Benson's ears pricked. The word 'cook' had a special meaning in cruising slang; it meant falsifying survey information. He'd heard stories, mainly from Cardinal, about crews who went out, and for one reason or another didn't do what they were supposed to. Sometimes it was occasioned by laziness. The crew blazed only the boundaries and lines of the survey area, sometimes not even that much. Then they sat around in camp and cooked up the plot information and topography maps. In other, rarer instances, the crews took bribes from the loggers, in order to make it appear that that there was less timber than there really was. That way the loggers had to pay the government less for the timber, particularly if they were in cahoots with the scalers who came in later to assess the number and size of the logs brought into the mills by the loggers.

Back in the tent, Benson asked Mackay what was going on. Mackay looked disgusted.

"The ranger told me that our estimates have been too high," he said. "Somebody in the government says that there's a lot less timber in here than we're saying there is. So they want the estimates cut by fifty percent."

"But you said that the timber here is some of the best you've ever seen."

"Well, the big boys don't agree. I'm just a dumb cruiser. They say its lousy timber, and if that's what they say, what the hell do I know?"

"What're you saying?" Benson asked. "That they're right and you're wrong? They've never been out here."

"They've been in the back room with the logging companies, I guess," Mackay said. "I haven't. I just take orders around here. And the ranger says that I'm going to be the head cook from here on in."

•

Two days later, the other experienced cruisers were transferred out and Benson was made a cruiser. They assigned a Greenie from the coast to be his assistant. Mackay stayed in camp with Ray, and they cooked the aerial survey information as it came in.

He was a cruiser now, but Benson wasn't too clear about what he was doing or why he was doing it. Ratson, the pilot who'd flown him in just a short time before, had been assigned to pilot one of the helicopters for the aerial flights, and he helped Benson out.

"You're taking your job too seriously, Greenie," he said. "Let's have some fun with it."

Ratson was a man who knew how to have fun. He soon found that a grizzly sow and her cub habitually fed in a moose meadow a few miles from camp, and he proceeded to drive the animal into a berserk rage by hovering just above its reach, then by buzzing it as it tried to herd its cub from the incomprehensible danger into the safety of the trees. Harassing the grizzly became a daily morning ritual, because the sow continued to occupy the meadow each morning. Ratson enjoyed animals. If they saw a moose, he chased it with the helicopter for as long as the animal would consent to run, and frightened moose run long distances. Everything he saw moving in the forest, Ratson went after.

With these kinds of distractions a matter of routine, Benson frequently lost track of what he was doing and even where he was. He had a hazy notion that he himself was supposed to be underestimating the timber, and so the data he passed onto Mackay, as often as not, was already falsified and frequently topographically incorrect. Ratson believed that a helicopter was meant to stay in the air, and he disliked landing it for any reason if it could be avoided, and he found ways to ignore Benson's requests that he be allowed to take the occasional plot. Soon most of what they did consisted of flying around looking for moose to chase.

Mackay didn't seem to care when Benson complained that Ratson wasn't letting him do his job. He dutifully cooked every sheet Benson and the others brought to him, and grew more morose each day. Cardinal, to lift his spirits, hatched a plan to snare an enormous bull moose that swam across the river about a mile above camp each day around noon. He built a raft and used it to hook a large and primitive lasso between two rocks in the stream, and he was more than a little surprised when the moose promptly swam directly into his trap. Without telling Mackay, he maneuvered the moose along the quarter mile stretch to camp by shifting the rope from tree to tree, keeping the bemused animal in a state of confusion until its tether range was no more than a dozen feet from the tents.

Everybody in camp thought it was a terrific joke except Mackay, who instantly recognized the problem it would create: sooner or later, the moose would have to go, and there was no way to release the animal without having it wreck the camp. So, in the absence of a solution, the moose stayed in camp, and the cruisers carefully stayed out of its way. Cardinal kept it fed, and, naming it after the chief of the Forest Service, made half-hearted attempts to tame it. The Greenies enjoyed it immensely, taking it all as a signal that they were in the wilderness, the true north strong and free.

Benson thought the moose was funny like everyone else did, but he also worried out loud to Mackay about what they would end up having to do to get rid of it.

"I dunno," said Mackay. "I suppose we'll have to pack up the whole camp if we release it, because the fucker will smash anything it can get at once it gets loose. It's going to be too risky to maneuver it out the way Ray brought it in because it's so pissed off it attacks anyone who gets near it. Even if we pack up the camp and we let it go, it might just hang around for days. I'll get Ratson to bring in a rifle next time he flies out for maintenance on the helicopter. We can shoot it and dump it in the river."

That wasn't to be. Two days later, the ranger drove into camp to check on the progress of the aerial survey. Unluckily he drove his truck right up to the moose and got out before he noticed it was there. Then he had to watch as the big bull reduced the vehicle to a battered pile of debris. The moose charged it again and again from all sides, its rage satisfied only when it managed to turn the truck on its side.

In a rage all his own, the ranger rejected Mackay's plan of shooting the moose and ordered that the camp be broken and moved and the moose released. He took the attitude that it was Mackay's responsibility, and when the camp had been torn down and carted to a safe distance, Mackay cut the rope holding the moose and swiftly retreated to the safety of a nearby tree. He spent nineteen hours there before the moose decided that his tormentors were defeated, and ambled off through the trees to swim across the river.

Cardinal didn't confess to having snared the moose, and nobody else would admit to the ranger who was responsible. So the ranger suspended Mackay. When he got a chance, Benson approached the ranger and tried to tell him that Mackay hadn't had anything to do with it.

"He damned well is responsible," the ranger told him, curtly.

"He's the senior man here, he's in charge of the aerial survey, and he has to take the blame."

Ratson flew Mackay back to Prince George. The Forest Service fired him, and another cruiser was brought in to take his place. The new man, sensing the difficulty of the situation, brought his own tent, pitched it at the edge of camp, and kept to himself. What had been fun turned into a business, not that Ratson stopped harassing his grizzly every morning, or that the crews stopped chasing whatever animals they saw instead of trying to fly accurate surveys. But Benson saw it differently. Someone he liked had gotten hurt, and the fun was suddenly artificial.

When Benson complained to Ratson that firing Mackay had been unfair, and that their aerial cruises were worthless and probably dishonest, Ratson set him straight.

"There's no point in doing accurate surveys," he told Benson. "It's all been worked out. There's no graft going on."

"Oh yeah," Benson replied, dubiously.

"Yeah. The government isn't going to log this timber. That's all been decided. They're going to drown it. The dam will be finished before anyone can build logging roads into here and set up mills. Then it would take years to log the valley. So what you're doing here is proving that the timber isn't good enough to log. The Forest Service probably doesn't agree, and they might not like it, but they work for the government, and what the government says, goes. They know. The dam is for the public good, and if a few trees get wasted, so what? We've got more than enough of them to last forever."

"What about Mackay?" Benson said. "Why does he have to be a victim?"

"Jesus," Ratson answered irritably. "The green stuff runs real deep in you, doesn't it? Victim-schmictim. You can't make an omelet without breaking a few eggs. Sure he's a victim. Cruisers are all going to be victims sooner or later. Cruising is too slow, and its easier to do it with airphotos and helicopters. In five or ten years there won't be any cruisers like him left anywhere."

Benson shrugged uncomfortably.

"Look," Ratson said, gesturing at the forest beyond the clearing they sat in. "There's going to be lots of victims around here.

There's about 5000 moose in this valley, and most of them are going to drown when the dam basin is filled. That old sow grizzly we buzz every morning is going to drown if she lives long enough. If you hang around whining about victims, you'll get yours too, sooner or later. So enjoy yourself."

Benson couldn't think of an answer. There didn't seem to be one.

•

He woke up in the middle of the night. Someone had brought in bananas in the last load of supplies, and the tent was filled with mosquitos. Benson listened to their light drone for a few minutes, then climbed from his cot, dressed, and walked outside. The moon was full, the air clear and luminous. He strolled down to the river and watched the moonlight play across the riffle, listening to the boulders bumping along in the fast-moving current. Off in the distance, he heard the roaring of a grizzly. It went on for a long time, and intermingled with the roars were other, odder sounds Benson couldn't identify. He went back to the tent disquieted, still wondering what was going on out there.

He found out the next morning when he and his greenie walked out to the helicopters with Ratson and the other crew.

"Jesus H. Christ!" Ratson mumbled, as they entered the clearing where the helicopters were parked.

Both of the machines were a tangle of wreckage. The cockpit bubbles were smashed and the tail sections pulled apart and scattered. The rotor on one of the aircraft had been broken off, and engine cowling and wiring ripped apart. In one place, a piston head was visible. Neither aircraft would fly again.

Benson's greenie turned to him. "Who the hell would do a thing like this?" he asked.

Benson grinned at Ratson. "It was your grizzly sow, right, Ratson? I guess she didn't like you interrupting her breakfast."

Ratson shrugged. "Doesn't much matter," he said. "The world's full of helicopters. But you'd better keep your trap shut about me buzzing that grizzly if you know what's good for you."

"The world's full of victims," Benson answered. "I ain't

129

planning to be one of them. But I'm sure going to enjoy watching you explain this to your big boys."

"I guess we don't work today," said Benson's greenie, not quite knowing what was going on. "What'll we do?"

"Oh, we'll find something to amuse you," Benson said. "Maybe we'll feed you to the grizzlies."

The Enemy Within

The war arrived in my town on a smoky day in August 1963 on the daily flight from the coast. The aircraft wasn't military, but it carried troops and it was an invasion just as surely as it was that September day in 1939 when the German Wehrmacht drove its tanks across the Polish borders to begin the last wholly visible war this planet will ever experience. The invasion of my town was different. It was wholly invisible.

The 1963 fire season was the worst in recent memory, and most of the able-bodied men in the territory were lost somewhere in the smoky afternoon fighting forest fires. Not that the invasion would have been any easier to recognize if they'd been at their normal occupations. The crimson sunset that night meant that the forests were burning, and that the destruction of the natural world was making of itself a beauty, a spectacle. People took thousands upon thousands of colour photographs, and a few of them are in the archives.

And there you have it. The complexity of the modern world. An invisible invasion, invisible invaders, invisible casualties, all of it obscured by smoke and fire that was as extraordinary to an outsider as it was commonplace to those who understood it.

On a much larger scale, the invasion was actually part of a mopping-up exercise, and the men who came in on the plane that afternoon knew it. The same battle had been fought and won across the continent, and there was no reason to think it would be any different here. The distances travelled were greater, sure, and the country was tougher, some of the people to be subjugated were wilder and more independent than in other places, but that would make no difference. Most of the industrialized world had fallen to the invaders with little more than a few whimpers, a few messy suicides, and an outbreak of trailer parks across the American sunbelt states. Notwithstanding, they had accomplished a social, political and economic reorganization so massive it was beyond the comprehension of those who directed it.

Members of the invasion force exchanged pleasantries as they disembarked into the haze, just as if they were tourists remarking on some piece of picture-postcard scenery. Few of them knew one another, although there was no explicit policy prohibiting fraternization. They understood that they had been sent to take over and reorganize specific sectors of the target community, and that their mission was more important and pleasurable than any old-fashioned notions of friends, community or human kindness. No other ethical instruction was needed.

Their first targets were in the lumber and food supply sectors. The strategy was to buy out the strongest independents, then squeeze out the weaker ones until ownership and control rested outside the community. The community could then be reorganized so that maximum profits could be extracted from both the community and the natural environment, and the populace manipulated into gratefully accepting whatever products might profit the invaders most.

The important thing at this stage was to remain invisible, and to accomplish this each individual in the strike force would have to be invisible even to each other. They might recognize the presence of kindred spirits, they might even acknowledge the solidarity of personal ambition that existed among them. But that was all. They were trained not to see beyond their immediate

132

focus, and indeed were chosen because they possessed that singular ability.

•

Glen Smith, from the Belgium Overseas Corporation, noted the smoky sky as he stepped through the door of the aircraft. He turned several times as he crossed the tarmac, sweeping his European-bought trench coat across the ground as he took in the panorama.

"Watch your coat there, chum," said a similarly-dressed man behind him. "It looks like it cost you a few bucks."

Smith grinned, not quite sheepishly, and bundled the coat beneath his arm without looking to see who had spoken to him. He entered the small terminal building, and then turned to his co-traveller and introduced himself. He almost didn't need to. The two men could have been one and the same. The other man, who happened also to be named Glen Smith, differed only in that he represented Dairy World, a conglomerate that had recently captured the greater part of the dairy industry.

"Looks like a war zone around here, doesn't it," said the Glen Smith from Dairy World, without a trace of irony in his voice.

"It does, a little," replied the Glen Smith from Belgium Overseas, which was an international lumber cartel. "Of course, it's fire season here, you know."

Glen Smith seemed momentarily interested. "Wasteful, isn't it? All those potential profits blowing on the wind."

Glen Smith shrugged. "This year is apparently worse than most," he said, with just the slightest hint of reassurance in his tone. "The resource can handle it."

The two men did share a taxi into town. Their conversation was rhetorical and not memorable. What they were seeing was not after all a city, small, ugly, and bursting at the seams, but a series of opportunities, ones that were still at the confidential stage. They stayed at the same hotel, recently built by a hotel chain headquartered in Los Angeles, but they did not make plans to meet later.

Let's ask some questions about our invisible war. Is it real? Where did it come from and why? Are the members of the invasion force evil? Did anyone resist them?

The invasion is real enough. If you don't believe me look at the storefronts the next time you drive down the street. How many of them are particular to wherever you are? Can you find another elsewhere in the same city, or in the next town? The people who work for them are different, it's true, but the uniforms they wear, brightly coloured and carefully unmilitary, assert a wholly military message. The banks and the multinationals all have new buildings and the newspapers, if they happen to still be locally owned, tell us that these organizations make too much money while everyone else goes broke. The invasion was and is real. But it's invisible.

I'm not sure where it comes from. If I were Kurt Vonnegut I would build a literary contraption out of it and make you laugh while you thought you understood what it is—some small corner of the heart of darkness. But, actually, this is the half-light of mediocrity and blind ambition in action. It is the Amway religion, Richard Nixon mixed with John Dean and G. Gordon Liddy. It is the EST Corporation. It is the independent self nestled as a functioning cell within a corporate body, no longer in need of individuation or particularity. It is Mount Ararat meeting the Tower of Babel. It is the whispering dollar, the rapist in the bushes, the middle-class functionary clicking open his valium container. And it doesn't matter where it comes from, because it is everywhere.

Is it evil? Well, Glen Smith is not an evil man. He is the man instructed to paint the sign on the gateway to Auschwitz, he is the mercenary who was beaten by his mother as a child, he is the Cambodian teenager denouncing his parents so he can enter the party cadres. He is a father of children, he is a breadwinner, he will buy his wife a small car and work for the charity of his choice. He is that part of the human being which craves the comfort of a will that is outside his understanding.

Is there resistance? Ah! The Resistance is a familiar and romantic configuration in the mind of anyone with a knowledge of that last visible war. One thinks of André Malraux facing execution in his role as Colonel Berger; one thinks of the cruel death of Jean Moulin at the hands of Klaus Barbie and the Gestapo; one thinks of stout peasants in berets fighting and dying in the mossy vineyards; one thinks of nervous intellectuals slipping from doorway to doorway in the chill Paris midnight. Planes fly over a grassy meadow in the darkness; packages of weapons are pushed out by parachute; one glimpses the tense face of a cultured British homosexual as he leaps from the open door of the aircraft, only to fall into the hands of the sadistic Nazi S.S. He is rescued by Simone de Beauvoir and her cohorts in navy turtleneck sweaters. Or he is not rescued. In either case he divulges no secrets, betrays no part of his God-given freedom-loving spirit.

In that world, evil is wholly visible, and goodness is likewise as substantial as the bread, cheese, and wine on the wooden table around which the Resistance meets each night. Every second person you meet is an artist or a writer, and at least one person in every cell will indubitably survive to record it all for history. Despite the dangers, you exist, the world exists, ideas exist. The Resistance exists. You are utterly secure. And it's time you woke up.

•

Mary Gelbart pushes a grocery cart along the aisle of the new supermarket in early August 1963. She is mildly dazzled by the sheer volume of merchandise available to her. She is not mistaking volume for variety, for in truth there is greater variety here than at the local grocery store where she has shopped for years. Only a small part of her is disturbed that nowhere in the array of goods at the supermarket is there a single item that she can say for sure has been produced by a human being she will ever see, meet, talk to. But then, this is a sign of progress.

Her disturbance soon fades. She is, in the argot, 'making a life', not participating in something that was once part and parcel of faith, hope and charity. If cornered, she will even admit her contempt for those concerns of so-called local self-interest. Everyone whines about progress when they find themselves falling under its wheels. Life is an opportunity, right? And you have to seize every opportunity you get, even if it's a small one. Nobody she knows would argue with that logic. Would you?

Her father fought in the war—in the infantry, she thinks, but isn't sure. Then they moved up north, because it was the land of opportunity, and when she finished high school she got married. She didn't marry a local boy, either. No sir. She wanted something better. Her husband runs his own construction business, and he's building houses for the newcomers so fast he'll be able to retire by the time he's forty-five. When that happens, they can move out of this town, with its smoke and fly ash in the summer and its 40-below winters. And who will blame them? This isn't exactly paradise.

Meanwhile, every penny counts, and if the prices in the new supermarket are cheaper, that's where she'll do her shopping from now on. If the local grocers go under, well, that's the way things are, isn't it? Progress means survival of the fittest.

Her husband, Bob, is the first to agree. "You gotta suck sloughwater for a while if you want to drink champagne," he says. His office is plastered with similar slogans.

He's a member of the local Golden Rule Drinking Club. They've playfully revised the ancient Christian motto to read: "If you have a friend who is loyal and true, screw him before he tries to screw you." He'll tell you that life is dog eat dog, and may the best man win. He cuts a few corners as a builder, but no one complains. They can, he says, always sell out with a profit if they don't like the house. He's a little nervous about the new contractors who are beginning to crowd him, backed as they are by the big companies. He knows that none of the locals are getting work building the branch plants that are springing up everywhere, but he says there's no profit in warehouse construction, that it's too tight-assed for him anyway, and that before the housing market slows down he'll be rich and long gone. And his wife can shop any goddamned place she chooses so long as he gets his meat and potatoes every night, and if she can save money doing it, so much the better. That's the way their partnership works, he says.

Glen Smith sits in the cramped inner office of the local dairy. On the wall behind him are two large photographs, one of the owner's family, and the other a picnic photograph of the dairy employees. On the whole, everyone in the two photos seems happy and interested in one another, in the things around them, and in the camera itself. The family photograph is a formal one; the members of the family all gaze happily at the father, who is after all the source of their well-being. He stares at the camera, composed and serious. In the photograph of the employees, several of them are laughing; one has an arm draped, buddy fashion, across the shoulders of his companions.

Glen Smith turns in his chair and counts the employees. Then he makes a swift calculation based on the information he's memorized about the annual sales of the dairy. There are nineteen people in the photograph. With a frown, he crosses out nine of them mentally. Another silent calculation, a smile of accomplishment, and another two cease to exist. The smile is still on his face when the owner of the dairy enters the small office.

"Sorry about the delay," he apologizes in a distracted shorthand. "Freezer unit on one of the trucks."

Without understanding the shorthand, Glen Smith assures him that his lateness is excused. "Please sit down," he says.

The owner frowns. The request that he sit down sounds almost like an order, and for as long as he can remember, giving orders has been his prerogative, at least in this office. He sits down.

"You've read the brief our people sent you," Smith says, exuding the confidence of the well-prepared. It is not a question but rather a statement of obvious fact. "So you have some idea of what I'd like to conclude in the next few days."

The owner, a stout, grey-haired man in his mid-fifties, gazes neutrally back at Smith across the cluttered desk. "I've been too busy to look at much of anything lately," he answers, in a tone that betrays that he knows exactly what is in the brief.

"Then let me summarize it for you," says Glen Smith, the friendliness in his voice edged with an authority that rejects the possibility of being trifled with. "I'll be frank, because I think

137

that you're a man who likes to get the straight goods. Dairy World is coming into this market. We can do it in a way that hurts no one, or we can, uh, do it the other way, so to speak."

The owner nods, maintaining his neutrality. "Go on," he says, making a small cathedral in front of him with his hands.

"We're a very large company." Glen Smith begins with a small sigh to indicate that he doesn't like having to say what he has to. He pulls an expensive pen from the lapel pocket of his suit and taps it absently on the desktop. "We can dump in this market below your production costs. And we can do it for as long as we need to. It won't hurt us at all, but it'll break you. We'll cut into your business and that will raise your costs again. I'm sure you can see the position you're in."

The owner destroys his finger cathedral, his hands flopping outward on his desk in an unconscious gesture of surrender. "Go on," he says.

"Listen," says Glen Smith, his tight grin breaking open expansively, as if to indicate that really, he's a reasonable sort of guy, dropping his pen on the desk to emphasize his own surrender to this reasonableness. "Of course we'd prefer not to take those kinds of measures. We're willing to pay approximate value for your equipment, and a generous price for your company's good will. You'll be a wealthy man."

The owner's hands go back to cathedral-making. He lifts his hands into the space between the two men and Glen Smith finds himself being stared at, momentarily, through the doors of a church. The hands come down to the desk top.

"I don't want to sell my business," the owner says quietly. "I've worked most of my life to make it what it is, and I love it. I've got employees to take care of."

"I'm afraid that we've all got to live in the real world," Glen Smith replies, cutting all warmth from his expression. "I don't think you're being realistic about this."

The owner merely sinks a little deeper into his chair.

"In any event," Glen Smith continues, brightening his voice, "We'll retain more than half your present employees. You understand we'll shift production to our main plant for reasons of efficiency. And with the economic boom, there will be lots of jobs available elsewhere for the ones we have to let go. If you fight us, we'll bring in our own people, and sooner or later you'll be putting all your people out of work."

The owner nods, and the cathedral crumbles a second time.

Glen Smith gets to his feet. "Please make an inventory of equipment, along with an estimate of normal stock levels. We'll bring in our assessors and use your documentation as the basis for our preliminary offer. I suggest you might want to obtain legal advice to ensure that you have peace of mind concerning the transfer documents."

Glen Smith extends his hand, but the owner remains in his chair without responding. "We'll be in touch with you in the very near future," says Glen Smith as he leaves the office.

•

Glen Smith ran into his counterpart from Belgium Overseas that evening in the lobby of their hotel. They exchanged greetings, but they did not share a drink together. Glen Smith flew out on the daily flight the next day. Glen Smith stayed on a few days longer.

That night a forest fire blew itself to within a few miles of town, and the next morning the streets were dusted with a blanket of ash, and a smoky haze swirled through the streets. The Forest Service was conscripting any able-bodied men they could find. It was not safe to be on the streets without having some clear and recognized purpose in being there. Everyone was saying it was one of the worst years they could recall since the war. Nobody asked Glen Smith to fight the forest fires.

•

A few months later Belgium Overseas outbid the local mills on a number of timber sales. There was a lot of talk about it, but mostly it was about the narrow margin of the upsets. Someone had given Belgium inside information. Most of the independent mill owners had different theories about who it was that provided the information. It was to be expected, they said. Those big boys

139

didn't get to be as big as they were by being dummies or straight shooters.

Before winter closed in, Belgium Overseas and several other big corporations began to buy out the independent mills at what everyone agreed were overly generous prices. A few independents refused to sell, and the word went out that those who didn't sell would lose their timber the next year by the same method Belgium had acquired its first timber sales. If that happened, of course, the mills of the independents wouldn't be worth scrap. To emphasize their power, Belgium Overseas bought out several of the major planer mills, closing some of them and using the others to hold the recalcitrant independents to volume contracts even when the prices fell—and the prices did fall because the big companies deliberately flooded the market.

Because of that a few more of the independents went under by the next summer. A few owners were bitter, but most were merely fatalistic. Progress is progress, they said, and no one can stand in its way. There was a lot of new money in town, fire season was on again, and Belgium Overseas was already consolidating its operations down on the river flats southwest of town, where they announced that they were building the Largest Mill in the World.

The dairy closed that summer, and Dairy World announced that it was building a new warehouse in the industrial park out on the river flats. They laid off eleven of the old dairy employees, and soon afterward fired two more for incompetence, bringing in people from head office to replace them. The old owner sold his house and moved down south.

Glen Smith came and went, always staying in the same hotel, where he was given a special rate. Other invaders moved into adjoining rooms on the same basis, and eventually they took over the entire third story of the building.

•

Winter came on that year with unusual fury. By November the forests were full of snow, the city streets spotted grey with fly ash from the mills, although Belgium Overseas had announced

140

that its new mill would reduce ash levels by 75% when it was in operation. And soon, their announcement seemed to imply, they would be about the only mill running.

Just before Christmas another planeload of invaders flew in. This time they had with them a flock of strutting politicians from the Capital. These politicians met with the local politicians at City Hall, and after no more than fifteen minutes the doors opened and the flock became quite a bit larger and they all strutted out of the council chambers together like a lot of overweight flamingos and called a press conference. At the press conference the Mayor stepped up to a microphone that the invaders had brought along just for the occasion, and smiled at the small group that made up the local press, and at the somewhat larger group of drunk loggers who were interested in any event that might get them some free drinks. Then he announced that Progress—with a capital 'P'—had arrived. They, and he stressed their unanimity with a lot of mutual handshaking and backslapping, were bringing the pulp and paper industry to the north. There would be not one but two mills built, and eventually, he said, there would be enough pulp mills to make everyone rich. A few of the independent mill owners could be heard groaning when they realized that they'd sold out far too cheaply, but that was drowned out by the cheers of the merchants who were expecting to get rich in the next few years.

Quite a number of those same merchants were heard groaning several weeks later when yet another planeload of invaders flew in to announce some further capital 'P' Progress, in the form of not one but two big new shopping centres that were going to be built on the edges of town. The shopping centres, they said, would provide an enlarged tax base for the city, and would bring to local consumers a new variety of merchandise and a degree of convenience heretofore unknown. They said that shoppers would be able to do all their buying without ever having to go outside the centres, and just like the planeload before them they stressed the magnitude of the profits involved and promised that everyone would get rich because of their development.

•

141

Now you know enough to recognize that I'm playing a game with you. You can see that there's no war going on here. This is merely a description, and an unfair one, of the recent evolution of business techniques, and the reorganization of our economic system into large, multifunctional corporations. There has been no mass destruction, no loss of personal property or fortunes, no outbreak of violence or disease, and almost no loss of life, right? There's nothing sinister or illegal going on here. And nothing to object to, except maybe a few suicides of people who aren't flexible enough to live with progress. Hell, a lot of people have gotten wealthy, haven't they? And isn't that what life is all about?

And that talk about the Resistance is a lot of nonsense. It isn't appropriate here. What's the matter, the taste of gravy too rich for you?

What can I say? Should I tell you that the Resistance is like the war—invisible? Should I admit that a few chronically unemployed drunks hooked themselves up with an off-the-wall agent provocateur who'd infiltrated a leftist splinter group, and that they attempted to torch the hotel the same night the pulp mills were announced and that both the second and third floors were filled with invaders and their puffed-up strutting political flamingos, and that all that happened was that the drunks set fire to the agent provocateur, who ran screaming down the hallways of the hotel with his back a mass of flames until Glen Smith threw a blanket over him and the other Glen Smith doused the remaining flames with a fire extinguisher, and that subsequently the government screwed up on the heroism awards the two men were promised by getting confused about who was who, and that somebody resolved it by deciding that there was only one man involved, thus touching off a public Alphonse and Gaston drill between the two Glen Smiths in front of the local television cameras, and that the story got all the way to the national news before somebody in authority stopped it. How embarrassing for everyone. Or should you perhaps look about you for your own evidence of resistance?

There's an old man drunk and unconscious in the doorway of that boarded-up store on the main street of town. He used to work at the dairy, which was torn down a long time ago to make way for a public parkade. Nobody uses the parkade, because it isn't safe to go in there, particularly late at night. He sleeps in the parkade at night, actually, safe there because even the muggers know there's no profit to be gained in robbing a hobo.

Just the other day one of the guys who got put out of work in the latest round of layoffs at the pulp mills got knifed by an unemployed logger. The pulp mill worker was driving taxi, and it was his first day. He had trouble finding the trailer park the logger wanted to go to, and the logger, as he put it in the preliminary trial, 'blew his top' and rammed the knife into the pulp mill worker's eyesocket. Then he pulled him over the seat and slit his throat.

Well, unemployment is a fact of life now, the government tells us. And all you have to do is look to see that the forests are coming down a lot faster than they're going up. Not many of those jobs that have disappeared have much chance of coming back.

Mary Gelbart is still in town, still shopping at the supermarkets for her groceries. Nowadays she drives out to the new centre at the outskirts of town where they've got a bulk foods outlet. Everything is mechanized, and she has to pack her own groceries, but the bargains are great, she says, and you can spend your whole day in the mall picking up bargains. Her husband Bob went broke about ten years back, and because most of the houses he built are falling apart, he hasn't had much success getting started again. So he drives a grader during the summer for the Highways Department, and a snowplow during the winter. He gets by, and he still goes drinking with his pals from the Modified Golden Rule Club. A few other things got modified along the way: they drink more than they used to, and they do more bitching about the sad state of the economy and less laughing about how much money they're making. And last winter Bob's best friend went home after a meeting, put his car in the garage like he always did and closed the door like he always did. Then he got back in the car and started it up.

•

About the only thing that hasn't changed much is fire season.

143

That happens every year, just like always. The fires aren't so big as they once were, but they make up for that in numbers. There's no timber left close to town so the fires don't burn in so close as they once did. There always seem to be a few days in August when the smoke closes in and drifts through the streets in memoriam. But nobody bothers to take pictures of it, because this is the future and everybody is about as rich as they're going to get and things can only go downhill from here.

Hanging In

"So," says Al the Barber, moving to slip the cover around Big Ed's neck, "what's the story here?"

At first, Ed, who looks like he's been run over by a gravel truck, just slaps his plaster-encased right forearm down on the arm of the barber's chair and grunts.

"He ain't gonna tell us," someone chuckles from behind a magazine. "Must be a sad story."

Ed looks up, grunts again, then grins. "Get stuffed, turkey," he says. "I don't need your cockeyed wit. I guess I'll have to break your poor little hearts."

Al isn't about to let this one get away. He has instincts, and that's one reason why his barber shop is always full of customers. Right now his instincts tell him he's got a good story sitting in the chair. Hey, it's hunting season, always a good time for stories, and Big Ed is about equally well-known for his hunting and for his bullshit. Normally Ed would be bullshitting about the moose he just missed, or bragging about the one he just got. Al steps in front of Ed, looks him over.

"Well," he drawls, "It's a sure bet nobody'd want to send you to the taxidermist the way you look. What happened? The wife beat up on you again?"

Ed's wife is about three feet tall and doesn't have a mean bone in her body except maybe Ed's on Saturday night, and everybody laughs like hell. Ed laughs, too.

"It's kind of a dumb story," he says slowly. "You know Bob Elson, eh? Well, we were up the Buckhorn in that old International he's got, headed for Wansa Lake. We're just tooling along, you know, looking. I got my .306 and he's got that crummy little 30-30 of his, and they're both sitting propped up on the seat between us like a couple of hunting dogs and we've got a jug there and we're working away on that.

"So we see this moose walk out of the bushes about 200 yards ahead, eh? So we stop the truck and hop out and it just stands there watching us. We both sight up, and we fire at the same time, and naturally the moose drops. We know we hit him good, so we start ambling down the road toward it like a couple of duffers out for a stroll. But all of a sudden the damned thing jumps up and heads right for us, right? So we start shooting at it *again* and we must have hit it four or five more times before it gets to us because we can see the pops of blood and hide as the bullets hit. But the fucker doesn't go down. It just about runs us over as a matter of fact, goes right past us and veers off into the bushes. You could see it had this crazy look in its eyes when it passed by, sort of halfway between 'I gotta get someplace fast' and 'Christ does this ever hurt'. We're kind of amazed, you know, and we watch it disappear into the trees before we wake up and start chasing it, right?"

By this time Big Ed has everybody in the place sitting still, except Al and his partner, who go right on cutting hair. If they stopped for every good story they heard they'd go broke in a hurry. Besides, there's no telling what you can pull off in the middle of a good story. One time Al gave a guy a pigshave for a joke and twenty bucks, while the guy who was paying for the prank sat in the other chair and told the victim a story about a guy who was given a pigshave by a barber and didn't know it was happening until it was done. Ed horks an oyster from his throat into

146

his mouth, rolls it around on his tongue for a moment and swallows it, then goes on with his story.

"So I gotta stop at the truck because I only had five cartridges in the chamber when I started, and I pull a full box off the seat and I'm running along ramming cartridges into the breech one by one and firing as I go. And I'm dinging the moose, far as I can see, because it staggers every time one hits him. But he's still going. Elson's way ahead of me, and he's running through the bushes about fifty feet behind the moose, firing from the hip just like the Rifleman. He's hitting it too. So we keep going, because the moose won't fall down. We're getting a fair distance into the bush by now too, maybe about half a mile or more. Then we lose sight of it when it heads down into a swamp, and suddenly we can't hear a thing."

Al touches one of the cuts that cover Ed's neck, and Big Ed winces and glares at him. Al shrugs, and Ed continues with the story.

"So we follow the trail of gore from the moose down to the swamp, and when we get down to the edge, there's the goddamn moose standing in a foot of water about 30 feet away, staring at us with this bright red beard hanging off his chin. His eyes have these little 'x's in them, and we both know he's almost gone. I'm about to blast him one more time when he sort of shakes his head at us like he was saying, 'that's enough', and he drops

"We go over to him and count thirty-four slug holes in the carcass. The meat was so buggered up we just left him there."

Ed is silent for a minute, as if he's still wondering whether it might not have been worth dragging the carcass back up the hill after all.

"So how'd you get trashed?" Al asks.

Ed scowls. "Hold yer horses." he says. "That's only half the story."

Al rolls his eyes, and the crowd in the barber shop, which is now standing room only, laughs.

"So we were sloshing around in the water there, poking at all the bullet holes in the carcass, and trying to figure out how the Christ the bugger could've kept going so long with that many holes in him. So I happen to look out across the swamp and goddamned if there isn't another moose watching us calm as you please, cropping lily pads. It's a bull, and he's got the biggest rack on him I've ever seen in my life. He's close to 200 yards away, but without even thinking, I brought the .306 up and fired. This bugger just drops in its tracks, right there in about two feet of water.''

"So this time we're wise, right? We reload both the rifles, and we edge along the swamp, ready to plug the sucker again right behind the shoulderblades if it moves. But this fucker doesn't stir, doesn't move a muscle. So we wade into the water to drag it in to shore. We get right up to it, and Elson and I are both relaxed and talking about how weird it is that this one drops so easy when it's twice as big as the other one, eh, and goddamned if it doesn't jump up and take off on us. And I don't think at all, I just decide that this one ain't getting away and I grab it by the antlers.''

"Well, off we go. I figure it ain't going to go more than a few yards and I guess it thinks it's heading for the hospital in Williams Lake, because it makes beeline for a stand of small spruce that runs up the slope from the swamp. I keep hanging on, and it goes right through them, mowing down trees that are six inches across the butt as if they were toothpicks. Of course Elson can't do bugger-all because I'm on the moose, and I'm not thinking about anything except that I better hang on for dear life. But I can see the timber's getting heavier, and sure enough the old bull krangs right into a spruce tree about three feet around and I go over the antlers and into the tree. So when Elson gets to us there's the dead moose at the base of the tree and I'm hanging off the lowest branch out cold, and he can't tell which one of us has the most blood on him—me or the moose. He says it's a good thing I wasn't moving cause he might have plugged me by mistake.''

Al finishes cutting Ed's hair, and everybody gets a good laugh when Elson walks in and tells everyone he's gotta take Big Ed to the Compensation Board and claim he fell into the gravel-crusher. If Ed can get time off they'll just shut the crusher down and the two of them can go hunting. They're still after a moose. But Elson says that this time they're just going to shoot it, because Ed's finally figured out that moose are for killing, not for riding.

Uniforms

None of that bunch ever kept a job for long. You might have said they didn't want jobs, and they would have said they didn't see the point of them. Bob would have told you his old man had a job once, that back in the old days, he actually owned a small mill. Leon's old man used to work for him, as a matter of fact, at least until the day a 2x12 spun off the greenchain too fast and caught him just above the knees. According to Leon, when they let him out of the hospital Bob's old man said he was too old and too gibbled up to work anymore, and so he went down to the nearest bar and stayed there. About two weeks later they found him face down in the slough south of town.

Bob's old man worked his mill as both sawyer and millwright for nearly twenty years. But when the big companies came in he sold out like everyone else did. After that, he didn't give a shit any longer, just like Leon's old man. He got drunk one afternoon and stayed that way for most of eight years, until his liver gave out.

Frank and Weasel weren't local guys. Like a lot of other

people, they came out of nowhere when the economic boom got going; drifted in one day looking to score, sucked in by the undertow of the big development promises. No one really knew how it was they got teamed up with Bob and Leon, just that they had, and that they'd stuck together. And Frank and Weasel didn't talk about where they'd come from any more than they talked about where they were going.

The four of them were among the meanest shitkickers in town, and they rarely missed an opportunity to show just how mean they could be. If you got into a fight with one of them you had to take them all on. And usually, that meant together, not one at a time like in the old days. Leon, skinny Leon with the bad teeth, started most of the fights.

He had a strange sense of humour, that boy. He got his best laughs out of bashing guys who wore business suits. He figured, he said, that even if he lost the fight he could always manage to rip up the guy's suit some. If he was around, Weasel helped out, and after a while he enjoyed bashing the suits every bit as much as Leon. He was adroit at grabbing the rear flaps of a suit jacket from behind and ripping it up the back while Leon held the guy by the lapels.

"What the hell," Bob used to say. "I had a dog once who couldn't pass up the mailman. Those guys ain't no different. They just don't like uniforms."

Actually, none of the four liked people in uniforms very much, Bob included. And when they ran into one in a bar, it meant trouble for the uniform and whoever was inside it. Maybe it wasn't just that the four of them were mean guys. Maybe it had something to do with the fact that the cops were always looking for them, and if they weren't, the sheriffs were, and if they weren't, the mailman was delivering some letter they didn't want to know about.

Business suits were the most complicated kind of uniforms for them, actually. Maybe that's why they went after that kind so viciously. With ordinary uniforms, you knew where the guy wearing it was coming from, and usually you knew why. And except for the cops, most of the time a guy wearing a uniform will go out of his way to avoid trouble. He's usually just a working stiff, and getting punched out isn't something he considers part of his job. But guys who wore suits were different, just like the big companies that were taking over everything were different.

In the old days you could work for a couple of months at somebody's gypo mill, and then go on a drunk for as long as the money lasted. When you came back still half-pissed and sick, they'd dry you out and put you back to work. But if you quit like that on the big new mills, some guy wearing a suit up in the personnel department would blackball you, telling you they wanted more stable people in their workforce and don't come around here again unless you want trouble with the security guards. And as the big companies picked off the gypo mills one after another, there were fewer and fewer jobs and more and more suits giving you forms to fill out and putting black marks beside your name.

Leon and Weasel were little guys who had trouble getting work, and they soon gave up altogether. They spent their time sitting around in their old rented shack down by the river getting drunk and sick and getting meaner by the day. Both of them did a stretch or two in the jail up on the hill above town, and more than once the charge that sent them up was assault. Jail didn't help their dispositions much, even though they dried out some and got fed properly for a few weeks.

Frank and Bob, by contrast, were big and healthy, and they could nearly always get some kind of work if they wanted it, driving truck or at worst unloading boxcars for the railway. But Frank had his own mean streak, and it got him on a lot of private and public shit lists and kept him there. If he wasn't arguing with the foreman, he was punching out the boss or the shop steward or stealing tools from the guys he worked with. Bob trusted him, but that was because the two of them had had it out a few times, and each time Bob had come out the winner. That was the kind of authority Frank respected.

Bob was different from the other three. He wasn't mean when he was on his own, and he wasn't a dummy either. Most people who knew him couldn't figure why he hung out with the others—after all, they never did a thing for him except get him into trouble. Of course nobody ever talked to him about it, and, well, maybe he just liked drinking and fighting and chasing women.

Frank was about the only guy in town who could keep up with him, and he'd grown up with Leon, so he sort of felt responsible for him. And if you took Leon, you got the Weasel with him. The book on Bob was that he'd straighten out sooner or later, get married and settle down. People figured that when that happened, the other three would go somewhere else, preferably to another town.

It didn't happen quite the way people figured it would. One summer night Leon and Weasel put the boots to a suit outside one of the bars. There was nothing unusual about that, except that about half an hour later six security beefos showed up at the bar and dragged Leon and Weasel outside. Bob wasn't around that night, but Frank was, and when he went out to help his buddies, the beefos jumped on him and broke both his wrists and most of the bones in his face. When he got out of the hospital, there was something different about him, and it didn't have anything to do with his rearranged face. Frank had gone silent and cold, as if the mean streak had broken loose inside him and was eating away at him. He stopped tearing around, and even gave up fighting. But he didn't stop drinking. He gave up working and moved in with Leon and Weasel, and spent his days walking along the trails beside the river, and his nights he didn't spend at all; he just drank them into oblivion.

Now, the reason Bob hadn't been in the bar that night with them was because he'd fallen in love, just like everyone said he would. The woman he fell for didn't fit people's notion of the perfect wife, though. Her name was Miranda and she was one of the strippers at the bar where the boys got into most of their fights. And sure enough, before the end of the summer Bob and Miranda drove down to the coast and got married.

She turned up pregnant soon after they came back from their honeymoon, and Bob got himself a serious job at one of the new pulp mills outside town, working night shift as one of their maintenance mechanics.

Things went just fine for them until the baby was born. There was something wrong with it, and about three weeks later, it died without ever coming home from the hospital. After that, Miranda sat around the trailer all day and watched television. The doctors

152

gave her a lot of pills and she took so many of them she was too stoned to cook or do housework. Bob tried to get himself transferred to day shift so they could live a normal kind of life, but the suits out at the mill wouldn't go for that, and he quit. He stayed around the trailer with Miranda for a few weeks but eventually the money ran out, and Miranda wasn't exactly great company because she didn't stop taking the pills. Jobs had gotten hard to find, so Bob went back to unloading boxcars.

He got Frank working with him, and before long he was hanging around with the guys again. Late one night Frank came over to the trailer in a real black mood and said the cops had thrown Leon and Weasel into the clink again. The two of them talked for a while outside the trailer, and then they got into Bob's pickup truck and drove down to the police station to try to get Leon and Weasel out. The cops told them to piss off or they'd end up spending the night with their friends.

So they gave up, and since they still had the case of beer Frank had brought with him, they drove around town and drank it. For some reason no one could figure out, Bob let Frank drive the pickup even though Frank'd been drinking heavily since about noon, and about 2 a.m. Frank chickened a cop car at 70 mph out on the road to the pulp mill. Frank lost, even though it was the cop that veered off at the last moment. As the cop car went by it swerved back and clipped the rear end of the truck, and both cars went off the road.

●

The cop survived the wreck, but Frank and Bob drowned when the pickup went over an embankment and landed upside down in one of the mill's effluent ponds.

Leon and Weasel were at the funeral, and so was what was left of Bob's family. His sisters were there with his mother, but she was too drunk to know what was going on. Miranda was there too, but she was so bombed on tranquillizers she didn't know what was happening either. So the two women sat there together in the front pew, their faces empty and bloated, not singing the hymns and not responding to any of the platitudes the minister was slinging. After it was over and the coffins were rolled away to be incinerated, people left the two women there to listen to the rumble of the furnaces. And they just sat there like it was the symphony until Leon came back in a taxi and took them home.

About a month later, Miranda disappeared into thin air, left the trailer door wide open and all her clothes stacked in a big heap on top of the bed, even her old stripper's costume. Some people figured that she'd jumped off the bridge but the police didn't bother to drag the river for her body. They said she'd run off, and privately a few people said she'd pumped so much crap into her brain that she just lifted off and drifted away.

Leon and Weasel hung around town for a while longer, but things didn't go too well for them with Bob and Frank dead. The cops put a beating on them whenever they screwed up, and then the suits down at the welfare office said they were able-bodied men and cut them off, even though they were on every employment blacklist in the area. And then one day Leon and Weasel were gone too. Nobody knew where they went, and no one wanted to know. No one at all.

Helen of Ilium

They started talking about Helen the day Wilbur brought her home to Ilium. Maybe it was because Ilium was a small town and there wasn't much else to do but work and raise kids and talk. Maybe it was something about Ilium itself, with its ancient mill surrounded by dilapidated company houses on one side and the wind whistling off the lake on the other. Maybe it was because Helen was different, new, and therefore worthy of attention. Whatever it was, from the day she appeared until the day she left for good, she was the centre of conversation for the whole town.

Wilbur was the foreman at the mill, like his father had been before him. He was tall and strong and quiet, and he'd grown up in one of the houses across from the mill. He came from a big clan, and he had kin—high, low and indifferent—just about everywhere you'd care to look. Most of them were of the low and indifferent variety, but there were enough of them that were good people, particularly around Ilium, that Wilbur never had to look far for a good meal or a card game or a little bit of conversation.

Maybe that was why he married Helen. Most people married locally, but Wilbur was related to so damned many people he had to find a real outsider. And the way he did it was unusual, to say the least. He'd gone to Las Vegas for a holiday during spring breakup, and he'd come back two weeks later, newly married, with Helen.

At first people assumed that she must have been some kind of showgirl, even though she didn't look or act like their idea of a showgirl. She was pretty enough, but she wore no makeup, she didn't have an American accent, and she didn't put on any airs. Some of the men insisted that Wilbur won her in a poker game down there, but they didn't insist very hard and that rumour didn't last long before the wind blew it out into the trees. People found that Helen was cheerful and friendly, and she had a way of treating people that made it impossible for them to dislike her even if they tried to.

Nobody did, and it wasn't long before she knew everyone in town by their first name: man, woman, or child. She even knew the names of all their dogs, and made a point of fussing over them whenever she went over to visit someone. That friendliness of hers took the edge off the rumours, although some of the women, when they'd gotten a few drinks in them, would point out that while Helen seemed to know everything about everyone, information on who she was and where she'd come from was still scarce as hen's teeth.

Every afternoon as Wilbur's shift ended, Helen walked down to the dock to meet him, picking her way through the ever-present mud and debris of the landing as if she were strolling through an exotic garden. People liked that. Wilbur wasn't much of a talker, and since Helen rarely spoke about herself, these public meetings were the only way people had of gauging how they were getting along. If Helen threw her arms around Wilbur and kissed him, things were going well. If she hung back, scratching an elbow and frowning as if she were discussing some disputed point of domestic business with him, well, maybe things weren't going so well.

Even after their daughter was born, Helen continued to come down to meet him after work. The child was born in the fall,

156

and through the winter she bundled the baby up each afternoon in a backpack and made her way through the snowdrifts, braving the chill winds coming off the lake.

When she got pregnant a second time, however, the visits to the mill ceased abruptly. Someone heard that the second pregnancy hadn't been planned, and that Wilbur wasn't exactly pleased about it. A few people, walking by the couple's house late at night, said they heard Helen and Wilbur arguing, and a woman said that Helen had come for a visit and had broken into tears for no reason. But nobody really knew what the problem was, if there was one at all.

There must have been a pretty large problem, because Wilbur took off a few weeks after the second child—also a girl—was born. He didn't come back, either. The strange thing about it was the way Helen took it. Most of her friends said that Wilbur was a rotten shit and that she was better off in the long run; what good is a man who can't handle his responsibilities? When they said it to her face, she just smiled and agreed that she was better off, but she never agreed that Wilbur was a shit. Instead, she went out of her way to mention the things about him that were good. He was troubled, she said, and he was having a hard time growing up. If it was a sunny day, or if she was feeling good, she would say "someday," and then sigh, leaving the rest unsaid.

The truth was that she really wasn't all that badly off. When Wilbur ran out on her he left the pickup in the yard and he left the bank account. Both were in good condition. Of course the house belonged to the company just like all the houses in town did, but there was an old and unspoken understanding with the mill-owner about widows. Desertion, like death or accident, was included in the definition of what made a widow. She kept the house without having to pay any rent.

Helen didn't have any relatives of her own, but that didn't matter. Before he disappeared, Wilbur made sure his family were going take care of Helen and the babies. And because Ilium was a small town all their friends helped out, without having to be asked and without self-congratulation. In a small town, helping out your neighbour wasn't charity. It was the best kind of insurance you could get. One of Wilbur's friends dropped off a load of firewood from the mill whenever Helen needed it, and there were free clothes for the kids and plenty of free babysitters, not that there was anywhere to go without driving the thirty miles of rough road to Prince George.

For a year or so, Helen just put her head down and survived, kept the kids well-fed and clean and the house warm and reasonably orderly. She did a lot of walking, not down to the mill as before, but out in the criss-cross of old Indian trails that ran along the lake. When people asked about it, she just laughed and said she was out visiting with the wind.

But most of the time, she was busy. She baked bread for half a dozen families, and she became, by default, den mother for the younger men at the mill, going so far as to take a first-aid course in town so she could act as a nurse in emergencies. Some of the young guys got together and bought her an old deep-freeze, which they kept full of moosemeat even out of season, and pretty soon every Sunday night there was a big dinner at her house that they all tried to get invited to. Helen was still a young woman, remember, and she was attractive enough to turn heads whenever she was in town. She was tall and strong, and she had the kind of good looks that people describe as handsome, maybe because she always knew where she was going and never hesitated about it, striding through the streets in blue jeans and a pair of hiking boots with her auburn hair streaming out behind her like a horse's mane.

Most of the young men from the mill would have loved to get into bed with her, but they soon learned that the only way to approach Helen was through the front door. One or two of the bolder ones came right out and asked her, and she smiled and turned them all down as casually as if she were refusing a cup of coffee. That just wasn't one of the things she needed, and she let them know she didn't need them in a way that also told them that if the time came that she did, she'd let them know. Few propositioned her twice, and no one really resented her for turning them down.

But it was a small mill town, and it wasn't long before there was trouble. After dinner one night, two of her young men began brawling on the road outside her house. It was apparent that they were fighting over Helen, and so she decided that it was her job to stop them. She took Wilbur's old baseball bat out of the closet, and calmly walked down to the road. She watched the two men circle one another for a moment, and then, very calmly she asked them to stop. When they ignored her, she made it an order. When both responded to that by trying to knock the other one's brains out, she brought the baseball bat down across the wrist of the nearest fighter. He wore a cast on his arm for two months, and although he was proud of it, and everyone knew how he'd gotten it, he wasn't invited back for dinner. By itself, that put an end to most of the fighting, at least around Helen's place.

After that, if the young bucks wanted to fight over her, they fought somewhere that didn't afford her an opportunity to intercede. They continued to want her, and so of course they continued to come around whenever she'd let them, doing their fighting elsewhere. But this story isn't about men, or about male aggression and asininity. If Helen had an opinion on any of those subjects, she kept it to herself, although it's safe enough to imagine that fifteen years later, and in a different place, she might carry the now-familiar phalanx of attitudes about the general intelligence of males and their treatment of women.

As it was, everyone in Ilium expected that sooner or later Helen would bed down with somebody, and an ongoing topic of conversation was about who it would be and who appeared to have the inside track at any given moment. Women are women, the men said; a woman needs a man in country like this. Most of the women agreed, but they didn't talk about it quite that way. Early on, Helen had made it clear that married men weren't welcome in her house unless they were accompanied by their wives. Thus free of any threat, the women of Ilium regarded Helen with a mixture of curiosity and slight envy. They took a subtle pride in her independence, and secretly hoped it would continue. And for several years, Helen nurtured her two growing daughters, slept alone, and listened to the sleek young bucks bellow and dance in the darkness beneath her window, apparently content with the clamour of their attention, and willing to put up with the occasional distant clatter of their colliding antlers.

When someone finally did move in with her, it took everybody by surprise. It wasn't a man she took in, but a couple, Clarry and Donna O'Donnell. Donna was an obscure relative of Wilbur's from the east, and her husband, Clarry, for sure didn't cut much of a figure as a man. He was a paraplegic, paralyzed from the waist down in a car accident. They were nice enough people, and Donna was nearly as pretty as Helen in her own way. She was petite and blond. Clarry wouldn't have been much bigger if he could have stood up for measuring, which of course he wasn't about to do.

About this time, Wagner, the mill owner, took to visiting Helen's place, and she his. That got the tongues wagging, and the question that came up most frequently after the one about whether or not Helen was sleeping with him, was whether she was going to marry him. Wagner was in his fifties, a widower, and he was worth a fortune. Maybe, the more cynical locals speculated, she'd waited around so long because she wanted more than free rent. And the young bucks stopped coming around, not wanting to lock antlers with the boss. But a month or so after Donna and Clarry moved in, Wagner stopped coming around.

A few months after that, someone noticed that Helen was getting a little bit thick around the middle. One of the female cooks up at the company cookshack who knew her well asked her point-blank if she was up the stump, as she put it. And Helen, with an odd smile on her face, admitted that she was.

Every single person in Ilium knew about it within three hours. Everyone assumed that it was Wagner's child, and as if to confirm this, Wagner showed up at Helen's that evening. A crowd formed outside on the road—people eager to see what was going to happen next. There was a lot of shouting from inside the house, and after fifteen or twenty minutes, he came storming out the door, and without saying a word to anyone Wagner climbed into his Cadillac and drove off, looking as cold and frozen as death itself.

Nothing happened for a few days, and then one of the company bookkeepers came over to Helen's and dropped off a letter saying she had to move out of the house. That brought the bucks back out of the underbrush. The next afternoon they went on a wildcat strike. Wagner came down to the mill and pointed out

160

that they had no business walking off the job on an issue that didn't have anything to do with the mill. Then he warned them that if it continued, he'd shut down the mill. Helen walked down from her place right after Wagner left and talked to a few of the young men, telling them she didn't want any trouble. She'd been thinking of moving out of Ilium anyway, she said, and they shouldn't go to so much trouble over her because it wasn't going to do any good for any of them. Then she started to say something else, decided against it, and walked back home with a troubled look on her face. That afternoon, she and Donna packed the kids in the car and drove the dusty thirty miles into Prince George to look for a new place.

When they returned, just after dusk, Clarry wasn't there. He'd gotten used to wheeling himself up and down the roads, so at first they weren't that worried. But after an hour, he still hadn't returned, and Helen went looking for him at the neighbours. He wasn't there, and none of them had seen him go by. At that news, Helen seemed frightened, and took off in the direction of Wagner's house, which was over on the far side of the lake. They heard her return a short time later—Wagner had left town that afternoon.

Someone found Clarry's wheelchair down on the company dock the next morning. The police came out and dragged the lake for the body. The foreman closed the mill for the day, and at least half the people in town went down to watch. But there was no body to be found.

"He'll come up sooner or later if he's there," the police told the crowd. "They always do."

Helen and Donna stayed around for a week or two. At first people asked them if they needed anything, but they said no, they were fine, and that they were moving into town at the end of the month.

No body appeared in the lake, and Helen and Donna left Ilium. It wasn't a month later that an announcement was made that the mill was closing down permanently. No reason for the closure was given.

That set the rumours flying, of course. Someone had heard that the Forest Service had tried to force Wagner to do more reforestation, and that he'd refused, closing the mill as a protest against the threat of increased stumpage fees. Someone else said that Wagner was running out of timber, but that, everyone agreed, was obviously bullshit. The mill was an old one, and a few people said that it had become too inefficient to run at a profit, and the timber was getting too far away to make modernizing the equipment worthwhile. And quite a few people said it was because Helen wouldn't marry Wagner.

Whatever the reason was, the mill closed down. A few of the old-timers stayed in their houses because, they said, there wasn't anywhere else to go. One of these days, they insisted, the mill would reopen. But one morning the town was swarming with uniformed bailiffs. The company, said the sheets of official-looking paper they handed out, was giving them just three days to move out of their houses. The same day, some Cat drivers showed up and bulldozed the buildings that were already empty, reminding the squatters that they were coming back in three days to knock down the rest, whether they were empty or not. Helen's old place, the house that Wilbur had grown up in, was the first one they bulldozed.

The people of Ilium scattered all over the country after that with their theories about why the mill closed, about what happened to Clarry, and about Helen. Someone claimed they'd seen Clarry walking around inside the house without his wheelchair a few days before he disappeared, and another woman said she'd seen Helen and Donna through a window just before they left. They'd been kissing, she said, and it wasn't sisterly.

Helen and Donna took the kids and moved away, and a rumour spread that they were living together down at the coast. Another rumour said that she'd found Wilbur, and that they were together again. But after a while, there was only the wind at Ilium.

The Fate of White-Tailed Deer

Benson woke up abruptly from his nap. Outside, the dusty logging camp, the dirty windows of the shack above his bunk, the close heat of the summer dusk, the grating whine of saws from the mill across the log-strewn landing.

It had not been a pleasant dream he'd been having, and he was covered with streaky sweat. There had been an assembly line, gears, conveyor belts, huge sawblades. And beyond that, the lush green of the bush Benson had worked in all day.

As the images faded, Benson realized that he'd slept through supper. He shook his head to clear it of the dream. That was more important. He wasn't really hungry. On the porch of the bunkhouse, he heard the men he worked with. They were drinking coffee and shooting at tin cans with small-bore rifles. Benson climbed out of his bunk, picked up a book, looked at the cover without reading its title. Then he threw it on his bunk and went outside.

One of the men, a burly faller with thinning blond hair, was putting on a sharpshooting display, blowing the filtertips off cigarettes from a distance of almost fifty feet. The .22 he used was his own, a hand-modified semi-automatic with a sawed-off butt and a barrel roughly ten inches long. Benson watched the faller as he popped the tips from several cigarettes in quick succession. The faller completed his volley with a quick high laugh, twirling the gun, pistol fashion, around his finger. There was a moment of silence, and then one of the men asked him where he'd gotten it and why he carried it in a jerry-rigged holster whenever he went into the bush to work.

"I modified it myself," the faller said, settling back against the step to signal that he was prepared to stop shooting and start talking. "About four years ago a friend of mine and I were falling some timber out near Wansa Mountain."

He lit a cigarette, and flipped the match squarely into the centre of a puddle of dark water by the side of the porch. He took a luxurious drag from the cigarette and continued.

"We'd gone out at first light, and as we were walking into the section we were cutting I noticed he had a white snot-rag hanging from his back pocket. He always used them, and I often kidded him about his finicky habits, needing a clean hanky and a ten minute crap every morning before he'd put on his pants. So this particular morning I didn't think much about the snot-rag being there. We were sitting in some underbrush about a hundred yards from the road having a cup of coffee before we started up the chain saws. We were just sitting there, talking quietly, about the weather or something like that.

"We finished the coffee and when my pal stood up, he bent over to put his thermos back in his lunch pail. That was when things got weird. What we didn't know was that some yahoo American hunters had been watching the patch of underbrush we were sitting in, and when my pal stood up like that, the Yankees spotted the hankie, and they must have mistaken it for the ass end of a white-tailed deer. Anyway, they started firing at us. The first shot plugged my pal right up the ass, and he fell down screaming bloody murder. I started hollering too as soon as I realized what'd happened, because I could see my best friend lying on his face in the underbrush with blood spurting out of his asshole. But the louder we yelled the more the hunters fired at us, and I ended up having to crawl out of there and across the underbrush for about 100 yards waving my vest in the air before they stopped shooting. By the time they stopped, that fucking vest looked like it was made out of swiss cheese.''

He took another drag on the cigarette and his audience waited for him to complete the story. He got up and turned his back to them.

"So I realized right then and there that if I'd had a gun on me, I could've fired a couple of rounds back in their direction and they'd have stopped in a hurry. Ever since then,'' he said, turning around to face them, "I've carried a gun whenever I go into the bush.''

"What about the guy you were with?'' Benson asked. "Did he die?''

"Nope,'' said the faller. "But pretty damn near. He ain't working in the bush any more, and he walks like he's got a broomstick stuck up his gig. He doesn't use hankies any more, either, at least not for snot-rags.''

"What about the Yankees?'' someone asked. "What happened to them?''

The faller shrugged. "They were just dumb assholes, that's all, out brush-shooting. They weren't trying to do us in deliberately, and they were apologetic as hell. As a matter of fact they drove us into town. After we got my pal to the hospital the cops came over and they had to explain what they were doing out there. I think they charged them with something, but nothing much came of it.''

He let out a short, brutal laugh, and sat down next to Benson. "Maybe they skipped out, who knows? If you're going to have hunters running around they're going to shoot somebody sooner or later. They get out in the bush and get skunked for a couple of days and they'll shoot at anything.''

Benson had heard similar stories, most of them true to some degree, and he heard close to a dozen more in the next hour or so. He leaned against the wall of the bunkhouse and let himself be warmed by the evening sun, listening. The loggers traded stories, and popped away at different targets with their rifles. Benson didn't believe or disbelieve what they said. Most of the stories, he recognized, were about how tough or smart the storyteller was. Men talked like that. There was nothing profound about it, and none of the stories he heard, except the one the blond faller had begun with, seemed to have anything to do with the kinds of questions that nagged at Benson. And he wasn't sure why that one story caught at him.

As the shadows deepened, he caught the blond faller staring at him. He smiled back at him skeptically, as if to assure the faller he was not completely taken in by what he was hearing.

"You know," the faller said to him, "you Forest Service turkeys should be carrying guns. You're more likely to get shot at than anyone."

"Why is that?" Benson asked, disturbed. One of the reasons he'd joined the Forest Service was so he wouldn't have to worry about things like that.

"You're out there all the time, and when you work you don't make much noise. Some of those crazies could be tracking you figuring you were a game animal, and without you knowing about it."

"If I carried a gun I'd spend all my time worrying about getting into a shoot-out," Benson said, more firmly than he felt. "No way."

"You ever fired a gun?" the faller asked, sweeping aside Benson's argument before he could formulate it further.

"Sure," Benson answered without certainty. It was true that he'd fired a gun. He hadn't been able to hit anything, and the kick suggested to him that the rifle had a life of its own. Benson hadn't liked the sensation.

"Let's see you shoot," the faller said, handing his gun to Benson, who proceeded to miss each target the faller pointed out for him.

"You're doing it wrong," the faller said, when Benson handed the empty gun back to him. "You're looking at the gun, and then at the target. What you have to do is put the two together. Watch."

About thirty feet away, someone had impaled a pinup from *Playboy* magazine against a tree. The faller fired at it and a small hole appeared where the model's head had been.

"Once you start seeing the target clearly," the faller said, "the

166

gun becomes part of your concentration. You have to see what it is you're shooting at. You've got to see it exactly, and as nothing but a target."

Benson took the rifle once more, and carefully squeezed off one shot after another, this time with slightly better results. The gun still felt foreign to him, and it made him uneasy to look at the photograph of the model in the way he'd been instructed to. It was no longer the representation of a human being, or even a piece of shiny paper. It was now the focus of a very peculiar and slightly uncomfortable sort of attention. But Benson had to admit he experienced a very real pleasure when he began to hit the target.

"You have to see what it is you're shooting at," the faller repeated, almost intimately this time. "You've got to see it exactly, and as nothing but a target."

Benson fired off several more rounds, and as he did, he turned what the faller was saying over in his mind. If everything was this easy, he thought, life would be simple.   ·

•

Before he turned in that evening, he walked over to the cook shack for a snack. A forest fire haze filtered the moonlight, filling the night sky with milky light. The mill was on night shift, and the high-pitched scream of the saws mingled with the deeper hum of the diesels across the dark clearing. Benson sat on the step of the cook shack for a few minutes before going inside. For once, his mind was empty.

Inside, he cut himself an oversized piece of pie and poured a cup of oily coffee under the watchful eye of the cook.

"I see you were taking lessons from Bullseye," the cook said with a friendly chuckle. The cook was the oldest man in camp, and normally, he was untalkative and bad-tempered.

"Bullseye?" Benson frowned. He hadn't heard the nickname, though it seemed appropriate enough. "Yeah, I guess. He sure knows guns, doesn't he?"

"He's good," said the cook in the same friendly tone. "But don't believe everything he tells you."

167

"Why not?"

"Well," the cook drawled, relishing what he knew and intent on stretching out his explanation as long as possible, "you know that story he tells about them Yankee hunters shooting his best friend?"

"Yeah," Benson admitted. "He told me about it."

"There weren't no Yankee hunters," he laughed. "He and his pal were out hunting together, and it was him who did the ass-shooting."

"No shit? You mean he really shot his own partner by mistake?"

"Yup." The cook was grinning. "The cops damn near charged him for it, too. Seems they were both sleeping with the same woman at the time. The guy he shot still claims that it wasn't an accident."

Benson flinched. "Do you really think he deliberately shot his own best friend? He doesn't seem like that kind of guy."

"I dunno," the cook said, moving his hands up and down as if they were scales and he was balancing an elusive truth on them. "He's a nice enough guy. But I don't go hunting with him."

Benson finished the pie and coffee in silence, said goodnight to the cook, and walked outside. The air was full of smoke and the whine from the saws pulled at his nerves. As he walked back to the bunkhouse he found himself wondering what white-tailed deer dreamt about when they slept, and if they slept at all.

Brief Romance

Benson could see that Spike was losing control of himself, and he watched without much hope as his friend tried to maintain it. But insult after insult swept across him like waves breaking over a wall. Spike was slipping, and Benson knew it when he saw his face begin to convulse and twist with the waves, saw his hands clench and let go, clench and let go.

Both of them knew who was baiting Spike, but only Benson could actually see Ray Reese. Spike was sitting with his back to Ray, and when he stayed that way, refusing to respond, the insults altered in variety as they grew in intensity.

Everybody in the cafe knew what was up, and each person had their own hopes about what would happen next. Nearly everyone, except Spike and maybe Benson, wanted to see a fight.

If Spike turned around, the fight would be on. So he kept his back turned and tried to sit tight, staring at Benson while Benson watched Reese.

"Keep your eyes on that maniac," Spike said. "If he moves, you jump."

"I know what to do," Benson answered quietly, trying to sound more certain than he felt.

But the instant Benson spoke, Spike, as if triggered by the words, broke and turned around, climbing from the booth in the same motion. The volume and pitch of the insults increased again as Reese scrambled from his own booth toward Spike. But when he drew close, Spike lunged at him, missed, and Reese back-pedalled, suddenly silent, shadow-boxing erratically. It was a fight now, no getting out of it.

The owner of the cafe, sensing what could happen to his property if the fight took place in the cafe, hollered "OUTSIDE!" Without turning his back on Spike, Reese slipped toward the door, and Spike moved to follow. Benson caught at Spike's arm, but Spike brushed him away, muttering and angry, and pushed through the crowd in the aisle, kicking the door open with a bang.

It was dark outside, but the parking lot was brightly lit by the familiar green mercury lamps on the street corner. Reese was waiting in the middle of the lot, grinning and waving his arms and shuffling his feet in complicated patterns, dancing.

Benson followed Spike, feeling more curiosity than fear for his friend. He knew Spike wasn't in much danger. He was big and an excellent fighter, while Reese was short and squat, a fighter too, but the kind who just liked to fight for the hell of it, usually picking on guys who were bigger than he was. He lost most of his fights, and he didn't seem to care. If anything frightened Benson in all this, it was that strange willingness of Reese's to get beaten up. What was he doing it for?

Nearly every person in the cafe had seen Reese in action at one time or another, and several had fought him themselves. There wasn't any uncertainty here, only action. Spike was going to win the fight and they all knew it. They were only curious about what exactly Spike would do to him.

In the parking lot the two men squared off. Spike, for all his anger, was like a stone, silent and still, waiting for Reese to make the first move. But Reese seemed content to dance, talking and cursing at Spike in a babble Benson couldn't make out. As he got close to them, Benson saw that his friend's face was flushed, and he heard him muttering under his breath. Then, as the

170

spectators formed a loose ring around the combatants, gleefully shouting encouragement, Benson saw tears in his friend's eyes.

Spike began to take off his jacket, and as he did Reese attacked, an old trick, and came in flailing, but Spike saw it and brought up a boot into his stomach. When Reese pitched forward Spike swung his right tearing the arm from the half-removed jacket catching Reese above the ear with a hard fist and Reese stumbled backward looked surprised and retreated a few steps, cursing.

Now Benson could hear what it was he was saying: Come on cocksucker come on come on ya fuckin gorilla ya hunka shit you wanna fight ya got one here ass sucker come on...

Spike attacked again snarling and weeping at the same time connected at least three times twice to Reese's head and Reese went down and came up again as quickly spitting blood and retreating, yelling louder, louder: YACOCKSUCKERCOMESUCKMYDICKMOTHERFUCKERMOTHERFUCKER COMEONMOTHERFUCKERCOMEONGETITHERECOCKSUCKERICANGIVEITTOYOUMOTHERFUCKER...

Spike hesitated, as if the barrage of words were a physical force, drew himself together and attacked. Reese turned to run but Spike's foot caught him square in the ass and he stumbled not falling because Spike was on him pummelling his back and head and Reese skittered away on his hands and knees thrashing the way a wolverine does, still roaring.

Benson saw Reese disappear among the spectators, scattering them, and the circle broke apart further when Spike picked up a block of concrete and threw it, missing Reese and bouncing it off the fender of somebody's new Ford. Benson glanced at the dented fender as Reese got to his feet, dancing again, then rolling back through the crowd toward Spike and the circle reformed. Reese charged with his head down and Spike hit him twice on the top of the head and he fell and Spike kicked him once twice caught him on the ear and Reese was up and running, away.

He turned and his face was bloody from the torn ear and he was still roaring: SUCKMYASSBIGBOYYOUCAN'TFIGHTMEYAPRICKLESSMOTHERFUCKERCOMEONCOMEONMOTHERFUCKEROUTHEREANDI'LLDOITTOYOUGOOD...

Spike charged at him again. Reese turned and ran, farther this time, out of the parking lot and into the centre of the intersection beyond. The oncoming cars pulled over and stopped, but kept their headlights on, turning their wheels so the lights were on Reese.

Reese stood motionless in the nexus of light, the blood streaming from his torn ear, screaming. Then he stopped, and there was silence. A car motor gunned, and someone in the crowd shouted "Finish it!" Benson looked around to see who had said it, but the crowd merely undulated anonymously.

Reese stood there for a long moment as if he were caught up in some dream that was purely his own, his face a brutal blank. Then, almost sleepily, he opened the fly of his pants, and exposed himself.

"SUCK ON THIS, YOU BASTARDS!" he howled. "SUCK ON THIS!"

There was a ripple in the crowd, and it seemed for a moment to Benson as if everyone might go after Reese. Then Spike ran across the distance that separated them, his arms out, now screaming too. But Reese was through fighting. He turned and disappeared into the thicket of poplars on the far side of the road as if he were a puff of smoke.

Spike stopped in the centre of the intersection in the spot where Reese had last stood, peering into the trees to see where his antagonist had gone. The crowd watched him until they heard the police sirens, and then dissolved into the cars, the alleys, or back into the cafe. Benson walked out into the street and stood beside his friend, but he could see nothing in the thicket. Reese was gone.

He took Spike by the arm, pulling him away, and they ran through the parking lot and down the alley to the small shack Benson lived in. Inside, they sat on the floor in the darkness, panting and listening to the police cars cruise up and down outside.

Spike was mumbling, and tears ran down his cheeks.

"He's crazy," he said, not really to Benson. "He's crazy he's crazyIwantedtokillhimIwantedohGodIwantedhimdeadhe'sgottobecrazy."

"You'd better keep it down," Benson said. "The cops will hear you."

172

Buquis

Andy told Benson about the wild man while they were in the truck on the way into town for the last time that season. It was just before freeze-up, and the crews were going in for a month of mapping while they waited for the bush to accumulate enough snow to make snowshoeing practical.

"It's time you found out a few of the really important things about working in the bush," he said.

Benson was more than prepared to listen. He'd grown to respect Andy in the last month or so, even though he didn't like him very much. At first he thought Andy was one of those guys who talk tough about everything, and Benson had had his fill of that. But Andy was different from most. Oh, he handed out his fair share of bullshit all right, but underneath it, he knew things about being in the bush. And he genuinely liked being there.

Benson had been working in the bush for five months, and that was just enough time to become overconfident. A few days before, Andy had deliberately let Benson get lost in a small area of bush just south of the lake they had boated up in order to cruise a patch

173

of prime timber. At quitting time one warm afternoon, Benson had suggested that they cross a ridge to get back to camp instead of walking around it as they'd been doing for the previous week.

"It's a lot shorter," Benson had said. Then he'd suggested that he cross it by himself, boasting that he could make it back to camp twenty minutes before the rest of the crew.

Andy had laughed—a rare thing for him—and told him he'd better stay with the crew. But after a moment's consideration, he reversed himself and suggested to Benson that crossing the hill might be educative.

"Give me your compass," he'd said. "It's just a short walk, so you won't be needing it."

Benson had handed over his compass and had headed cheerfully uphill into the dense bush of the ridge. Four hours later, just as dusk was falling, Andy came and got him, offering him neither sympathy nor an opportunity to make excuses. Benson didn't try to excuse himself. He'd gotten lost, and that was enough to keep his mind occupied. He couldn't have explained how it had happened, only that he'd never been more frightened in his life.

"Next time you won't be such a smartass," had been Andy's only comment.

•

"So what is this wild man?" Benson asked, leaning over the front seat of the truck.

Andy looked at him in the rear view mirror, as if judging the seriousness of his interest. "The Indians on the coast called it the Buquis," he said.

"This isn't some dumb bullshit about sasquatches, is it?" Benson asked.

"No, no. That's white man's stuff. The Buquis is what you saw when I let you get lost."

"I didn't *see* anything," Benson said. "I just got lost."

"Why did you get lost?" Andy asked, rhetorically.

Benson assumed that he was merely rubbing it in, and didn't try to hide his sense of humiliation.

"Stupidity," he admitted. "I let you take my compass off me, for one thing. I was overconfident. But I sure as hell didn't run into any wild man out there. I didn't run into anything at all."

"I guess you didn't," Andy said, staring at the road ahead.

"Was I supposed to see something?" Benson asked, after a moment. He wasn't the sort to believe in spooks. But then, he remembered, there was no reason for him to get lost walking across a simple hillside, and there was no reason why he'd panicked the way he'd done. Even as he was panicking he'd known what he should have been doing: sitting down, building a camp, staying in one place. But his mind had been divided, as if it were in two places at once. One part had been mocking him, reminding him that he was only crossing a dumb hillside. The mocking voice had told him it was simply a matter of continuing to walk in the direction he was going. Over the next dip. Here, there. Go this way, go that way, be tough. The other voice had welled up from deeper inside him, and it had told him to run, told him to stop, told him to hide, told him that what was happening shouldn't and couldn't be happening, and that something was very, very wrong with him.

"How many voices did you hear while you were getting lost?" Andy demanded, suddenly.

"Two," Benson answered without thinking.

Andy described the voices and precisely what they'd been saying. Benson tried unsuccessfully to hide his disquiet.

"There's always two voices," Andy explained. "One tells you to be more brave than you are. The other tells you to be more timid. It's the crossfire that gets you."

"How in hell do you know this?" Benson asked, incredulously.

"I *remember* it," Andy answered. "A guy did the same thing to me that I did to you. Years ago. I did it to you right on schedule, just like I do it to everyone who works for me. That way, when something really happens in the bush, you know what to do, and you stay alive."

Benson thought he'd known what to do before he'd gotten lost. Andy had told him that the day Benson had started working on his crew: don't give up your compass, and don't believe your senses when you're in the bush. Then he'd gotten mystical about

175

it. In the bush you are, he'd said, where you are first, and who you are comes second. And everything outside you is where it is first, and what it is comes second. When your senses start messing around with that formula, you have to remember where you are and you let your compass tell you where things are, and you forget about what they are and you forget about who you are.

It didn't seem so mystical now, and Benson realized that Andy never said anything that went beyond practical matters. So when he let Andy take his compass he lost the means to figure out where things were. And he lost track of where he was. But he still didn't quite get it.

"So what about this wild man?" he asked.

"Buquis. There's two of them. An aggressive one and a shy one. You didn't expect to see some monster covered with fur, did you? The bush isn't like it is in a Walt Disney movie."

Andy pointed to the road and then tapped his own skull. "It's out there. And in here. Balanced. If the balance breaks down, the Buquis gets you."

Benson still didn't quite understand. "I wasn't really that lost," he said. "I could have walked out in the morning."

Andy shrugged. "Maybe. But when I found you, you were lost."

•

After two weeks of drawing maps and studying other maps in the Forest Service offices, Benson began to get an inkling of what it was Andy was trying to tell him. One afternoon Andy walked in with some air photos and the stereoscopic lenses that give air-photos the illusion of depth.

"What're these for?" Benson asked when Andy dropped them on his table.

"I thought you might like to see how you got lost. These are the photos of the timber sale we worked on up there." He pawed through the photos, pulled two of them out and placed them side by side, placing the lenses over them. "Here's where you lost it. Have a look."

Benson lined up the registration marks and peered into the

lenses. It was all there: the boundary of the lake, the ridge, and the logging road that curved around part of it. At first, he couldn't see why he hadn't been able to simply walk over the ridge and out. But when he studied the terrain below the ridge, he noticed an undulation in it that curved first across it and then subtly curved back around on itself. At the top of the undulation, the timber was heavier, but that wasn't something you could see on the ground. The area enclosed by the circular undulation was less than half a square mile. It wasn't large enough for a reasonably experienced woodsman to get lost in, and yet that was what had happened. Benson never reached the top of the ridge. Instead, he'd followed the undulation, and had been walking around inside the bowl it created. He must have circled it several times, more than once crossing his own path.

•

The next morning the Chief Cruiser called all the crews, roughly twenty-five men, into a small meeting room.

"We've got a report of a lost American hunter," he told them. "He's been out there two days, near the edge of Wells-Gray Park. The police want us to go in and find him."

He waited for a moment before going on. Benson caught Andy's eye, and Andy winked at him. Benson had never been in that area, but he'd heard it was supposed to have some of the roughest terrain in the region.

"This isn't going to be a lark," the Chief Cruiser said. "That hunter, if he's alive at all, could be in very rough shape. He's supposed to have some survival equipment with him, but whether he knows how to use it is another question. If he'd used it properly, he wouldn't be lost."

The Chief Cruiser explained the search method: they would use four-man teams, working in pairs, compassing and ribboning long search lines, covering the area in a geometric grid until they ran across tracks. Once those were located, one pair would follow the tracks, accompanied by a second pair running compass lines on parallel.

It was mid-November and for a week it had been alternately

177

snowing and thawing. It was because of these conditions that the Forest Service crews were being brought in. Helicopters wouldn't be able to pick up the trail, and too many unskilled searchers would likely confuse or obliterate any tracks that were there. The Forest Service crews could pick up the trail on the ground, and follow it efficiently.

Within ninety minutes, the teams of searchers were equipped and on their way. Andy headed one of the teams, and Benson was on it.

"You've done this before, eh?" he asked Andy as the truck hurtled down the highway to the search site.

"Yeah. A couple of times."

"Did you find the guys?"

"Oh yeah."

"Alive?"

"Once or twice."

"You ever find one dead?"

"Uh huh."

"What was it like?" Benson asked.

Andy shrugged. "Let's just find this one and see how it goes," he said simply.

•

It was snowing lightly when they started their search pattern, compassing long lines across the hills and marking the lines with plastic dayglo ribbon. The snow was less than a foot deep, and the bush was eerily quiet. They returned to the road near dark having found nothing but a few moose and wolf trails. That night they stayed in a small motel near the search site, and long after everyone else had fallen into an exhausted sleep, Andy pored over the air photos he'd brought.

The next morning as the crews were preparing to leave the motel, Andy talked to the Chief Cruiser. Benson watched them talk, and when Andy got into the truck, there was a thin smile on his face.

"What was that all about?" Benson asked him as he started the truck.

"I was looking at the air photos last night."

"I saw you. Did you spot something?"

"Maybe," Andy answered grimly. "Maybe not. We'll see. We're going to a different location today."

Andy drove the truck several miles past their original search site, pulled off the road, parked, and the crew climbed out. A dusting of snow during the night had softened the landscape, and the eerie quiet was even more oppressive than the day before.

Benson took out his compass and sighted down the gentle slope, wondering what Andy had seen in the air photos. Andy walked over and stood beside him.

"Keep your eyes on your compass shots today," he said. "There's going to be some pretty funny turns out there. I want the lines straight as an arrow."

•

They were only a couple of miles into the bush before Andy found what he was looking for. Benson had walked right across them without seeing them, and had to be called back. The tracks were barely visible, but unmistakable just the same. Andy bent down and brushed the new snow out of them.

"What now?" Benson asked.

Andy didn't answer, continuing to poke into the snow around the tracks. Then he measured the distance between the indentations, and consulted his map. The other two men in the crew appeared, and Andy instructed them to compass a line: 120 chains south, double that east, then build a fire and wait. Benson realized that Andy expected to find something important inside the arc of that three mile distance, but before he could ask what it was, Andy answered his query.

"You and I are going to follow the trail," he said and began to track the footmarks toward a low ridge just ahead.

Benson followed a few steps behind him, feeling slightly apprehensive. When they reached the crest of the ridge, Andy stopped and let him come alongside.

"What's going on?" Benson asked.

"He's carrying a packsack, and probably a rifle, and he's tired,"

179

Andy said, pointing at the length of the footsteps. They were closer together than those of Benson or Andy. Benson had already noted that from time to time, the footsteps veered off to the right. From that, he deduced why Andy believed the walker was carrying a rifle.

From where they were, the terrain sloped gently down, but not sharply enough to provide any viewpoint of the landscape ahead. There was nothing to see but the dense and snow-dusted evergreens, and the faint trail. They began to follow it again, and when the slope bottomed out they found a packsack and the beginnings of a crude camp. A campfire had been attempted, unsuccessfully.

"This guy is no woodsman," Benson commented, pointing at the abundant and dry moosemoss in the lower branches of the trees. "I could've started a forest fire here."

Andy grunted as he rummaged through the lost hunter's packsack. "We'd better bring this with us," he said.

Benson shouldered the pack, and began to follow Andy once again. This time they walked for close to an hour in silence before Andy stopped.

"What is it?" Benson asked, wiping the sweat from his eyes. Andy's pace had been brutal.

"Look at this. He just crossed his own trail."

"What do we do?"

Andy looked up, as if surprised by the question. "We ignore the second trail. We're going to track this guy exactly as he came. If we don't, we'll only waste time, and I doubt if he's got much of it."

Benson nodded. That made sense.

•

"Won't be long now," Andy said, a few minutes later. They'd followed the trail until it circled back to where they'd seen it cross the original trail. Benson had had no sense of going in a circle.

"Shit," he said. "This is like what I was in, isn't it?"

"Yeah," Andy said. "I saw it in the air photos. He's in here somewhere. If he isn't, he'll have gotten out of it just west of where I sent the other guys. They'll pick up his trail if it comes through. But I don't think it will."

"Why?"

"Look at the tracks."

The trail had grown progressively more erratic, the footprints closer together and more slurred.

●

The two men followed the trail down to the floor of what Benson could now recognize as a bowl. He began to look more carefully at the timber, and he saw that it was smaller as they descended, turning to swamp scrub and muskeg. In the spring and summer, this would be a swamp.

They found the rifle beside the trail. There was no break in the tracks; it had simply been discarded. After that, the steps began to lengthen, until the distance between each one was more than double that of Andy's or Benson's. The man was running, obviously, flat out, and with an astounding agility.

Andy stopped, and Benson looked past him and saw why.

"There's our man," Andy said quietly. "Or what's left of him."

●

They walked toward the huddled figure. It was crouching, face down in the snow, with the buttocks sticking almost comically into the air. Andy circled the body, then pushed at the buttocks with his foot, and the body toppled stiffly onto its side. The eyes were open but opaque, the mouth a rictus grimace.

"Must have tripped," Andy said laconically, reaching down to check the dead man's pockets for identification. He removed a half-eaten chocolate bar, several rifle cartridges, and a compass. Andy fingered the compass, flipping up the metal cover. He balanced it in his hand.

"It works," he said, stuffing it into his pocket. Then he reached into his pack for the map. Benson watched as he traced his finger across its surface. Andy looked up.

181

"Go get the others," he said, pointing off through the trees. "They're over there someplace. And make sure you use your compass."

The Castle

Ozzy Schultz wasn't a pleasant guy. By the time he died he had more enemies than friends, and it'd been that way for a while. Come to think of it, by the time he died he had no friends at all. Over the years he'd stiffed quite a few of the local businessmen, and he had a habit of rubbing their noses in it once he'd done it. When he died most people said he deserved what he got, good riddance; and his creditors swarmed over the estate like flies on a carcass.

The big banks, and I'll be goddamned if I'll name them, put him in receivership for three million dollars worth of unsecured debts. He'd never liked lawyers, and he hadn't bothered to put all his companies at arm's length, and he'd recently fired his accountants. So when the banks went after him like that, they brought the whole damned shooting match down. That was the first surprise. Everybody was running around hooting about how all Ozzy's badass business practices had finally caught up with him and when they weren't hooting about him getting what he deserved, they were crying about how the bastard managed to

183

take them for one last ride. But his assets, when they were to-talled out, amounted to close to twenty million. Everybody got what was owed them.

Now, even a dumb old one-horse real estate salesman like me can see that there's something fishy going on when a man worth twenty million goes down over a debt that's less than a sixth of that. No way that should happen, no way on earth. The way I figure it the big breweries got into cahoots with the banks and put him down because they didn't like the way he was running that little brewery of his, making all kinds of different beer and selling it cheaper than they were. It was either that, or one of those big international construction companies wanted Ozzy out of the way. By the time he left town for good, they'd hired away all his best people and were overbidding contracts that had gone to him in the past. The union didn't mind, because Ozzy had always been a mean son-of-a-bitch to his operators, coming down to the jobsite and firing people just because he didn't like the look on their faces.

As a matter of fact he did just that to me once when I was younger. I'd stopped the Michigan loader I was running to have a smoke, and he caught me. Told me to get off his job if I thought smoking a cigarette was important enough for me to shut down my machine. "Go smoke all you want in the unemployment lineup," he said.

I didn't like him for it at the time, but it taught me a lesson. Deep down, I knew he was right. I also knew that if I'd been dumb enough to lip off to him when he fired me, he would have kicked my ass off the site all by himself. I saw him do it to other guys a couple of times, and he wasn't one to lose a fight. You didn't have to like Ozzy to work for him. What you did have to do was work for your paycheque, and unless you were a lazy good-for-nothing, you had to respect the man. I did, and I always sort of knew that I wasn't hearing the whole story when people started yapping about what a bad bastard he was.

The north country is full of guys who come out of nowhere and make good. Ozzy was one of them, maybe the biggest of them all. The local legend has it that he started off by buying an old cat and renting it out to the Forest Service for fire season. The

184

first thing he did when he got the cat near a decent-sized forest fire, the story goes, was to drive the worn-out hulk right into the middle of it. In those days, the only way the Forest Service could get cat operators to fight fires was by offering to replace any piece of equipment that got destroyed on the job with another one, same model, brand new. Ozzy got his new cat, and somehow he parlayed it into several more, picked up an old scraper and wangled some roadbuilding contracts out of the government. Pretty soon he was running the largest construction operation in the whole damned north country, bar none.

Even in the early days he had a talent for making enemies. One reason, for sure, had to do with him marrying Tishie Hanson right out from under the nose of old Hank Spar, the biggest lumberman in the area. Nobody could figure out what it was that Ozzy did to get her to break off her engagement with Spar, except that when they got back from the honeymoon her hair was bleached blond and she was driving a white Cadillac convertible, the only one in town. And she had a tan that never went away.

Her family and all her old friends were so pissed off about it that they wouldn't have anything to do with her. Maybe it was because she'd married Ozzy instead of Hank Spar, or maybe it was because of the white Cadillac, the bleached blond hair and the perpetual suntan, but nobody would invite her and Ozzy over for drinks or dinner. So she drove the Caddy around town all day picking up anybody who wanted a ride just so she'd have someone to talk to while Ozzy was working. Ozzy himself didn't seem to give a shit about being ostracized. He just kept working eighteen hours a day, and his companies got bigger and he got meaner and richer.

After a while, he bought 200 acres of land right on the outskirts of town. It cost him a fortune to get it, even though about half the land was supposed to be unbuildable because of the instability of the hills behind it. The first rumour was that he was going to build a subdivision up there, but then that changed when he hired an expensive architect from out of town. He was going to live there, the architect told the locals, and he was planning to build the biggest, fanciest house the town had ever seen. The local builders said he was crazier than a bedbug to build out there, because if he disturbed the hillside the whole thing would come down on him the first time it rained.

Ozzy contracted the house himself. When the rough details of how he planned to build the house came out, and what it would include, it was the biggest joke in town. Not only was he building the largest house the town had ever seen, but he was installing a 50,000 gallon swimming pool, and he was going to put it indoors so he and Tishie could swim in it, year round. The experienced contractors said there was no way a pool could be built up there. It wouldn't last a year, they said, before the underground springs in the hillside split it into small pieces.

When the cement trucks started going up there, the laughter died down a little, and when the trucks kept on going up there day after day, the laughter stopped altogether. Ozzy knew all about the instability of the hillside, of course, and what he was doing was filling in the whole sidehill with concrete. If a landslide came, it wasn't going to touch his house, and no underground spring was going to break up his pool. He poured a slab of concrete four feet thick for the house to sit on, and in some places, according to one of the labourers he hired to work on the pool, the concrete in the pool was ten or twelve feet thick.

He spared no expense on the house. He used solid walnut planks for panelling all through it, and built the kitchen out of real copper sheeting and pink Italian tiles, and installed every appliance he could think of. Then he put in purple wall-to-wall shag carpet through the rest of the house, the thickest anyone had ever seen, and had all the furniture hand-built out of solid walnut and covered in black and white leather. He had an intercom system put in, with speakers in every room. The house was about 5000 square feet in all, not counting the pool. And when it was finished, he and Tishie threw a party and invited damn near everyone in town.

Well, to cut a long story short, nearly everybody came to the party, and it was the biggest social disaster the town had ever seen. The first thing that went wrong was that a bunch of disgruntled subcontractors Ozzy had either refused to pay or somehow or other chiselled out of full payment came to the party and demanded that he pay them on the spot. Ozzy tried to be polite at first, but when that didn't work, he took the biggest contractor and threw him through one of the picture windows. Then he took a 2x4 and chased the rest of them off. One of the contractors leaped into his pickup, went careening backward down the long driveway and ran smack into the mayor's car. The mayor got a broken nose out of it, and had to be taken to the hospital.

It didn't get any better, either. Ozzy had a moose barbecuing in a big pit he'd had built out back against the sidehill, and the coals from the pit set fire to the underbrush. By the time anyone noticed it, a good portion of the sidehill was on fire. The fire department wasn't going to come out because it was outside the city limits, but Ozzy and some of his employees at the party managed to get it under control. The other guests did nothing. Led by Hank Spar, they stood around and watched.

Ozzy was enraged, and as far as I'm concerned, rightly so. Spar and his cronies had broken one of the unwritten laws of the north: nobody watches a forest fire, no matter how small. If you're there, you pitch in until the fire is out. When they got the fire out, Ozzy came back into the house, stripped to his shorts in front of Spar and the rest, and jumped into the pool. The others who'd been fighting the fire followed suit. They swam around together for a few minutes, and then Ozzy climbed out and walked over to where Hank was standing and hammered him right between the eyes. Knocked him cold, and took out about half his front teeth. Then Ozzy waded into the rest of them.

So the party ended in a brawl, Ozzy and his people against the locals. It could have gotten pretty dangerous, because there were a lot more locals there than Ozzy and his friends could handle. But most of the locals didn't have much stomach for the fight, probably because they were feeling guilty about having stood around while Ozzy and his men put the fire out, and enough of them took their wives and cleared out when the fighting started that Ozzy was more than able to hold his own. He got pretty badly beaten up, and the house was more or less wrecked, but after the locals left he and his men partied for two days in the rubble.

After the party, he closed up on the local business community, doing as little of his buying from town as he could, and making sure the new people he hired to work for him didn't come from town. When his construction crews had to shut down for the winter, he hired a whole hotel downtown for a weekend, and threw another party. It was Ozzy's revenge. When the party ended there wasn't much left of the hotel, or of the surrounding area.

•

The next spring he built a huge fence around the house, and put security guards on the front gate twenty-four hours a day. Tishie still drove around town in her white Caddy, but she didn't do any shopping in the stores any more. Trucks came straight from the coast to supply Ozzy's construction camps, and I guess Ozzy got his groceries that way. He flew his private plane down to the coast on business a lot, and more often than not, Tishie went with him, to shop and get her hair fixed.

Inside his tall fences Ozzy was up to something, because the construction equipment kept coming and going, and every so often a semitrailer would pull in and unload. Stories about what he was up to began to circulate, fueled mainly by kids, who looked on Ozzy's fences as a challenge. But the stories were so wild and various that no one took them seriously.

Another year went by before I became curious enough to take a look for myself. I had a reason. I'd stopped working in construction, and had taken a correspondence course in real estate. I did well enough that I'd passed the licencing exam with flying colours, and I was looking for a job. I figured that any inside information I could come up with would do me good. So I drove up to Ozzy's property late one afternoon to take a good look.

The fence he'd built was about ten feet high, and he'd built it out of split logs—big ones—that gave it the appearance of an old trading fort. The only things missing were the rifle turrets.

I took this as a sign that I wouldn't be shot if I climbed the fence for a look-see. I drove down to the far corner of it, as far from the gate as I could get, and parked. I pulled the stepladder I'd brought out of the back of the pickup, propped it against the fence, and climbed up.

Little more than two years had passed since Ozzy's party, but with the changes, it could have been 200 years. Along the entire lower perimeter of the fence, which was close to half a mile in length, was, so help me, an algae-filled moat, with canals penetrating the interior of the property, ending in what appeared to be beaver ponds. Most of the rest of it had been extensively landscaped; returned, artificially, to forest. The trees were mainly northern species common to the area, but here and there, and crowded by more vigorous plantings, were some exotic varieties I'd never seen before. The crowding of the exotics seemed so deliberate that it drew my attention to them. And here and there I saw several dense patches of devil's club, a plant common enough in the muskeg and wet uplands all over the north, but which had been more or less wiped out in the area around town.

But the weirdest part of it was the animals. There were beaver and ducks floating around on the ponds, and one or two moose fed on some lily pads. But there were more deer than anything else. They were everywhere, and I counted fifty of them in a small area near where I was.

They were easy to count because they didn't move. None of the animals moved. That was what was so weird—they weren't real. Not a goddamned one of them. They were all life-sized and life-like, but they weren't alive.

Well, I couldn't make sense of it. I stood there on the top of the ladder with my arms hooked around the top of the fence and gawked at the scene for about half an hour, trying to figure out what Ozzy was up to. But whatever it was, it was beyond me. In the distance, I could see the roof of the house, and through the trees, a glimmer of colour—an odd, almost neon orange-pink that was out of kilter with the rest of the out-of-kilter scene.

The moat curved around the corner of the property, and where the land sloped upward to the house and the hills behind it, I could see cement buttresses where the moat appeared to end. My curiosity had been pricked, and since I'd seen no movement anywhere in Ozzy's forest and heard no sounds, I assumed that there weren't any guard dogs around. I climbed down off the ladder, packed it over my shoulder and tramped along the fence to the corner, where I picked my way through the underbrush, following the fence until the ground began to rise and I knew I'd run out of moat. When I saw the tops of some trees close to the fence, I propped the ladder against it again and crawled up. On

189

the other side, the trees were so densely planted that I couldn't see more than a few feet into them, and, I decided, nothing and no one could see me. Straddling the top of the fence, I pulled the ladder up and over, then dropped it down on the other side and clambered down.

The ground was covered by a thick carpet of green moss, spongy and soft. I walked through it quietly toward the house and that patch of colour I'd seen, gingerly, because I expected my shoes to be getting soggy. I wasn't dressed for the occasion—I'd gone up for a look over the fence, not for a hike into the wilderness.

But the moss was quite dry, and I reached down and picked up a handful. It was made of some sort of synthetic material, the kind I'd seen before in the local flower shops. Now, as I looked at close range, the trees were fake too. Most of them. Here and there, pushing up through the plastic moss, were seedlings, and here and there were remnants of the lodgepole pines that'd been there when Ozzy bought the land. I guessed that Ozzy wanted his forest in a hurry, and this had been the only way he could get it. Whatever his logic, it was keeping my shoes dry.

Then the craziest thing of all happened—I got lost. If that sounds impossible, well, maybe it was. I wasn't leaving any tracks, and I couldn't exactly blaze trail on the plastic trees. I must have gotten down into a bowl in the centre of the area, one where I couldn't see any landmarks, and once in, I guess I did what a lot of people do—I circled the bowl again and again, confused by the anonymity of the landscape into believing I was walking in a straight line. The light made it worse. The sun had set behind the hill, and the failing twilight made definition impossible.

I didn't panic. That would have been completely ridiculous. At best, it would have brought Ozzy or his guards down on me, and I would have had to explain just exactly what I was doing in his plastic forest with my real estate card in my pocket and my new shoes, and my white shirt and tie. If the word got around town about that, I'd never live it down. The weather was good and the night air warm, so I pulled up a patch of the plastic moss, made a bed, and crawled in. It wasn't the first time I'd slept outdoors, but it felt strange to be doing it while I was sober.

I woke up at first light, hungry and a little chilled, but not so discouraged that I was willing to give up entirely. I still wanted to see what that patch of colour was, and I wanted to see what Ozzy's house looked like. I replaced the moss I'd pulled up, and judging the direction of the house from the light in the east, headed west. I fuddled around for an hour, and finally eluded the bowl that'd trapped me—not that I knew how or when I accomplished that. The trees began to thin, and ahead I caught a glimpse of that orange-pink colour.

I pushed my way out of the forest and found myself on the edge of a formal garden. That colour was from a flock—several hundred at least—of pink flamingos. All stationary, all plastic. I sat down on the moss and began to laugh.

"What's so funny?" I heard a female voice say.

No more than a dozen feet away, sitting in a lawn chair, was Tishie Schultz, her white blond hair cascading over her shoulders. She was wearing a white nightgown and pink mule slippers, and she was smoking a cigarette in an ivory holder. Paralyzed, I said nothing, watching the smoke from the cigarette drift up in the still air. I'd never actually seen her this close before. She looked older than I expected her to, her skin criss-crossed by wrinkles under the dark tan, and traces of black roots showed where her white hair met her scalp.

"Well?" she said. "Don't you think you'd better explain what you're doing here?"

"I got lost," I answered, blurting out the worst. "I spent the night down there somewhere." I pointed to the forest behind me.

It was her turn to laugh. "Oh, that," she said. "I'm glad to know it works. Ozzy said it would."

She stood up, suddenly serious. "This is private property," she said. "You could be prosecuted for trespassing. Or worse, if Ozzy were here."

"I was curious," I said, hoping to talk my way out of trouble. "I wanted to see if the rumours were true."

"And are they?" she said, her voice quiet.

"No," I admitted. "This is different. I don't understand what this is at all."

"I don't imagine you do."

"Well, why did you and Ozzy do this? It doesn't make sense."

She laughed. "Do the things you people do in town make sense? Have you had a close look at the city you're building? Or at the way you treat people?"

Before I could answer, she stood up and looked behind her as if she could hear someone coming. "You'd better leave. Where did you come in?"

I pointed behind me, south. "Over the fence. In that direction."

"There's a trail that leads to that part of the fence. You can follow that. Please don't come back."

She whirled around and disappeared along the same trail. I waited for a moment, then followed her footsteps until the trail forked. I could see the house through the trees, and I could hear her, because she was humming a tune. I took the other fork. Just as she'd said, it led to the fence, and I followed the fence until I found the ladder.

When I got back to my apartment I slept for about twelve hours straight. I didn't mention what I'd seen to anyone, not even when I was drunk.

•

Ozzy bought the town's small brewery shortly after that. It didn't seem like an important acquisition at the time, but it was probably that little brewery that led to his downfall. He pumped a lot of money into it, changed the brand name to 'Ozzy's' and then started doing the things that upset the big breweries, cutting prices and making new kinds of beer, mainly varieties that contained more alcohol. For a while he was making a high octane brand that had double the normal alcohol content. The government put a stop to that venture, and in the process turned Ozzy into a hero amongst beer drinkers all over the continent. It began when he started to appear on television and on radio talk shows, yakking about how his beer was a better buy and that he was just a little guy that the government and the multinationals were trying to screw. Soon the press created a full-blown myth around him that somehow caught the heartstrings of people from just about everywhere. Except, of course, in our town. The locals kept on ignoring him, and when they weren't doing that they were putting him down for being nothing but a dumb cat driver.

But while they were putting him down, Ozzy was putting the town on the map. It wasn't quite what the local politicians had in mind, either. They'd been touting the place as the White Spruce Capital of the World for years, and no one had been interested. Ozzy and his beer made the town the beer-guzzling, fist-fighting capital of the north, the best place around to get drunk and lie face-down in your own vomit; the A-1 spot to get your face rearranged in a hundred different ways and for a thousand different reasons; the home of Ozzy Schultz's 10% killer beer.

Television crews came in from all over, and the local loggers and construction workers obliged them by confirming the town's reputation at the drop of a hat, free of charge, any time, anywhere. And Ozzy was selling a lot of beer, even though he wasn't making much money on it. His freight costs were too high, and he wasn't selling much to the bars because they were all under contract to the big breweries, and that's where the profits lay. The local economy was going stale, and at the same time as that was happening, the construction industry was getting more competitive, with the big international companies moving in.

Meanwhile, I'd started with one of the real estate agencies, and without really knowing why or how, I was making a small fortune of my own.

Then, right out of the blue, Tishie walked out on Ozzy. Some people who claimed to have inside information said that things hadn't been going too well with them for a number of years. Ozzy, they said, wanted kids, but Tishie couldn't have them or something like that. Maybe she didn't want them. Anyway, she left. A rumour went around that she was seen driving south in the white Caddy, and that she'd had the top down and the car was packed with luggage.

Ozzy stayed on at the house for a while, and the word went out that he was up there doing nothing but getting drunk. I saw him in town one afternoon about that time, and he looked pretty rough—his skin all pasty-white and bloated. There were rumblings about his finances, and then he up and abandoned the whole thing, house and everything. Just walked out one morning, fired the security guards, left the house and the front gate wide open, got into his plane and flew to the coast for good.

About a month later they found him dead in his hotel room. It was a cheap hotel, and he'd had a heart attack some time during the night. For all the rumours that he was broke, he'd been keeping half a million dollars in cash in the hotel's small safe.

•

Well, the rest is history of course, a matter of public record. There's only a couple of things I want to add to that record. And I'm the only one who can do it, which is why I'm writing this.

The spring following Ozzy's death, I got a letter from a lawyer in Los Angeles instructing me, on Tishie Schultz's behalf, to put the house up for sale. There was a note from Tishie with it, sealed, and a cashier's cheque for five thousand dollars. The note was short and sweet. I was to get whatever I could for the house, but I was to ensure that all traces of the garden had been destroyed before anyone was let onto the property. The cheque was to pay for the costs of that. I would understand why it had to be destroyed, she said.

There wasn't anything left to destroy. Ozzy had bulldozed the whole damned thing a few nights after she left. He'd pushed all the fake animals and foliage into big pyres with a cat, and set fire to them. It was the goddamnedest stinking bonfire anyone had ever seen, and the fire department rushed up to the property to put it out, but Ozzy wouldn't let them in. There was a pall of black smoke hanging over the town for three days afterward. Besides Ozzy, and his security guards, I guess I was the only person in town who knew what he was doing. But I didn't talk about it. I was a businessman, and successful businessmen don't get to tell all the truth, particularly when it's the kind that no one would believe.

I listed the place, but it didn't sell. I knew that was going to happen, but I tried my best anyway. Eventually, I locked the place up, but within a year the drunks started using it as a place to crash in, and for a time a group of really strange hippies took it over and were out there taking drugs and holding orgies. As soon as I found out about that I had the police go up and clear them out, but there wasn't much left of the house to save by then. Over the winter the frost had cracked the pipes inside the floors, and the heating system was no good after that. Most of the doors had been kicked in, and the windows too, and the purple shag carpet looked like the hippies had been using it instead of the shitter. About the only thing that wasn't damaged was the pool. It was empty, the bottom littered with broken bottles and crap like that, but it was sound as a drum. Some of the furniture was still in the house, oddly enough, filthy but sound, and no one had bothered to pillage the bookcases, which were still full of books. Ozzy's choice of books kind of caught my eye one day while I was up there poking around. There were a number of Rosicrucian books, and I counted nineteen books on the same odd subject: how to attract good luck. I thumbed through several of them, and they all looked like they'd been carefully read. Some pages were earmarked, and passages had been underlined and annotated.

Over the fireplace, and untouched by the succeeding waves of vandals, was a huge framed photograph of a yellow D-9 caterpillar tractor. I stared at it for a minute, and then, on an impulse, lifted it from the wall. I guess I was looking for a wall safe. There were several in the house, all of them open and empty. There was no safe behind the photograph, but taped to the back of the frame was an envelope. It was blank, but there was a piece of paper inside it.

I opened it. After all, I was the real estate agent. But I felt guilty about it. I was hoping, I guess, that there was money in the envelope. Anyway, I read the piece of paper. It was handwritten by Ozzy, and here's what it said, word for word.

WHY I DID IT.

It looks like its just about over with me. The Bastards will get me one of these days anyway. Well I built it and I wrecked it. And why I did it is what I have to say in this letter. In the summer of 55 before we got married I was building logging roads east of town and on Sunday Tish come out. We took the powerboat upriver some, to the mouth of the McGregor. There was some low cloud on the North

195

side of the mouth and to throw a scare into her I ran the boat full blast into the middle of it. Thats how we found it, we rammed the sandbar and when we walked across it there it was.

It was a big mansion on an island, real old and made out of stone. It was bigger than anything in town. It looked as if someone was taking care of it but there wasnt nobody around except a bunch of deer and some flamingos running around. A lot of both. Some birds were there, singing all the time, but I couldnt see them. I went around looking at the foundations and Tish walked out back to a courtyard. I seen her talking to some woman with blond hair but afterwords she said she never saw anyone there. She packed a picnic for us before we come with a bottle of rye and some sandwiches and we sat in the dining room of the house all panelled in walnut, and ate our lunch and drank the rye. Tish was acting real funny and it was pretty spooky I admit it. So we left.

I wanted to go again but she wouldnt go along, so finally I went by myself. It was maybe two months later but there wasnt anything there the second time, just an old oxbow stuck in behind a thicket of willows. Where the house was there was just a grassy island with some more willow trees.

We got married and all. Right after that Tish changed. She got me to buy her a cadillac and she got her hair bleached. I figured O.K. with me because she looked real sharp, It'd make those Bastards pant and drool.

Then after that party where I nailed Spar she changed again. She wanted this fenced in garden with all the animals. So I checked around and figured I'd get this company stateside to supply everything. They did it in a hurry and that made Tish happy. When it was built she said she liked it because it was nice and clean. She got pretty strange, but I didn't argue. I mean, I worshipped that woman, like she was god to me. Whatever she wanted.

As long as I made money and left her alone she was happy. She never liked screwing much when we first got married but then I figured shed come around but she never did. So

I forced her a couple of times near the end, just because I couldnt stand it anymore. I guess thats why she took off. She said I was finished and that no man could give her what she wanted, it just wasnt possible in this hellhole. She said no one had ever understood what she was. Well I guess I didnt.

So after she left and all and I knew she wasnt ever coming back I bulldozed the garden and burned it. If anybody'd seen it they would have thought it was me who was crazy. But who cares who knows what now. If you ever wondered what that black smoke was for, it was for her and her garden.

Yours truly
Ozzy Schultz

That's more or less the story. The reason I'm writing it down is because I've had enough of this place myself. The real estate market has gone all to hell, and I'm broke. So I'm getting the hell out I don't know who I'll give this to, maybe nobody.

I never did sell Ozzy's house. I kept dropping the price, but nobody wanted it. For a while I considered bulldozing the building, but then I remembered the pool. You could drop an H-bomb on the place and that pool wouldn't budge.

I did cash the five thousand dollar cheque. Hell, I need the money. I spent some of it to pull down the fences, and I rented out some of the frontage land to one of the equipment companies. They're parking their burned out equipment on it, pirating the hulks for parts. The house is still there. It'll probably be standing on doomsday.

My Friends Are Gone

My name is Don Benson. Or at least that was my name when I still needed one. I never thought I'd end up as a historian, that's for sure. I only know bits and pieces of history, and what I do know is mainly local. I don't know much about literature, either. But I've seen some things, let me tell you, and lately I've been getting a few ideas, and they've stuck in my head. Can you understand that? There's no reason any more for writing anything down, except that if I don't, that's the end of it; nobody will ever know. And why shouldn't I? Not having a good reason has never stopped anyone else.

I was born here in the north, and I've lived here all my life. That in itself may be a special qualification. A lot of people came and went in the north, most of them staying just long enough to make enough bucks so they could go someplace where the winters aren't so cold and the summers last longer. At least, that's how it used to work. In the last decade or so, things have been a little different. People used to make their money and get out fast, but in recent times, the ambitious ones just left without making much, and the rest stayed and hung on.

When I was younger, I had some fuzzy ideas myself about living my life the same way most people did. But then one thing led to another, and I put off leaving. When the world started to get pretty rough a few years back, the economy here went to hell worse than in most places, and it was discovered, as if it were a huge surprise, that most of the good timber was gone. Pretty depressing stuff. I couldn't see it being any better anywhere else for me, so I stayed around. At least here, I was at home.

Something in the back of my mind started clicking, and it told me that things weren't ever going to get better, and that this was where I should be. Maybe it was because the north was all I knew, and maybe it was because the rest of the world was looking so ugly, and maybe it was because I figured that if I stayed here I wouldn't get nuked if the crazies went for it. I suppose it was a little of each of those. And maybe it was just lack of ambition.

When I was a kid back in the late 50s, I thought they were going to use the nukes then. Every kid did. A couple of my friends and I took it so seriously that we even planned out what we would do when it happened, thinking like most kids seem to have to, that we would be able to survive. We knew there was a nest of large caves near the lake east of town, so we scrounged a bunch of old camping equipment and canned food, and ditched it all at the back of one of the caves. It became our fallout shelter.

We were only thirteen or fourteen years old, but over a period of a year or so we managed to get a fair amount of equipment and food out that cave. We had our getaway route all planned out for when the attacks started, and for a couple of years we spent most of our spare time either transporting equipment out there or trying to make the cave liveable. Near the back of the cave there was a series of passages that ran deeper into the hill, and we traced these back to a spring. So we even had running water, and we made a rudimentary sewer system out of a natural sump hole we discovered deeper yet in the hillside. And we built some bunks and tables from trees we dragged in from outside.

Of course, there was no nuclear war, and the scare eventually eased. When it did we lost interest in the cave, mostly because we were growing older and there were other things to interest us closer to the surface, as it were. My friends forgot about the cave completely, and as soon as they finished school, they left town and didn't come back, just like most young people who grow up here. I stopped going out to the cave, but I didn't forget about it. It stayed in the back of my mind, like an insurance policy or one of those security blankets small kids have. There was a part of me that felt protected by its existence. The world couldn't get to me, nothing could, because I had a place to go, even if I never used it.

After I finished school, I had a lot of different kinds of jobs: I worked in a tire shop for a while, drove delivery trucks, worked for the Highways Department while they were still building roads. But mostly I worked for the Forest Service. It was an off-and-on thing. I was a cruiser for a while, and then I worked for Silviculture, marking the trees for the loggers to cut, and I did some smoke-jumping during the summers. Later on, I did a lot of tree planting, first as a Forest Service employee, and later, after the pulp mills came in and the Forest Service changed, I planted trees for the private contractors. For a few years I was even a contractor myself.

There was never much money in tree planting, unless you didn't give a damn about whether or not the seedlings survived. I did give a damn, and that was my biggest problem. Most crews went out, planted a few acres of seedlings properly, then pissed around, dropping the trees in without spading them up or sometimes not even bothering to plant them at all.

After a while I realized the government wasn't really trying to reforest, that they were doing only enough to convince the ecology freaks and the college-educated liberals from the big city that things were just fine out in the boondocks. The thing that finally convinced me the government wasn't serious about reforestation was when they started dropping the seedlings out of planes, by the thousands. About one in two hundred seedlings might make it that way, whereas if the seedlings were planted carefully, it would cost more, but forty or fifty percent might survive if the weather conditions were right. But the government was only interested in how many seedlings it could take from the nurseries and get rid of, because that was the way reforestation quotas were set. Ten million seedlings a year is an impressive number, even if they all end up drying out in the treetops or drowned in some swamp. It looks great in those bullshit annual reports the government puts out, but it doesn't mean they're putting living trees in the forest.

When I was running my own tree planting company I insisted on planting seedlings the right way, even though my crews didn't like it much. Doing it right was hard work, and none of us made much money. But I kept doing it that way, and as a result I barely made a living wage, because I had to bid against contractors who were willing to go out and dump the seedlings in the river if they could turn a profit.

I guess I decided that you can't cover up the fact that you're ripping people and things off, not forever anyway, when I saw what happened after the government filled up the dam basin on the Peace. The government claimed that as soon as the big lake filled up it would be usable for shipping and for recreation. But the first few times people took boats out on it, the vibrations from their motors loosened the drowned trees, and anywhere up to two or three hundred of them would come up at once underneath the boats. The lake was dead and useless. I never forgot that.

Eventually I got tagged as an oddball because I wouldn't go along with the system, and the tree planting contracts dried up. Private enterprise, they called it. What it meant was that when everyone is cheating, you get rewarded for aggressive cheating, and for looking and acting like everyone else. I wasn't ever one for drinking beer with the government supervisors, and for them that was more important than how I planted trees.

I'm not whining about it, though. I knew how things were, and it seemed to me that there was nothing to do but pay the price for doing things right. I didn't need much to live on, and I wanted to be outdoors, and planting trees was about the only way to keep on living the way I wanted to. The other contractors would always hire me on to plant the small plots of legitimate planting they used to show to the government supervisors, or to the ecologists who occasionally came snooping around.

I never got married. I could see the way things were going, and there was no way I was going to bring a child into that kind

202

of mess. It was hard at first, but after a while I began to prefer my own company, and the loneliness stopped bothering me.

●

So that's who I am. The next question, and maybe it's the only question left in the world, is why did it happen. Well, I don't know the answer. Sometimes I think it happened because we used up the resources, and life got too hard for the people in charge, and they were too lazy and stupid to change. And maybe the ones who might have changed things were too comfortable, too compromised to be courageous. I can't tell you that for sure. I can only tell you what happened around here, and what happened to me.

I remember the seventieth anniversary of the founding of the town. The mayor and a couple of ex-mayors got together and cooked up a big announcement, congratulating the residents (who they called 'the voters' because that was the only use they had for them) for voting for them all those years, and for having progressed as far as they had. Then they predicted a bright future for the place, just like they always did. About half the people were out of work at the time, most of the mills were shut down and nearly all the mines, and no new construction was on the books. The downtown looked like a ghost town, old newspapers and dust blowing up against the boarded up stores. The only reason anyone went down there was to get drunk, or get laid, or get into a fight. Or to catch a bus out. Those mayors couldn't or wouldn't see that the fun was over.

The shopping centres out in the suburbs still did a good business, but I rarely went out there myself. The few times I did I could never find the things I wanted, just a lot of imported junk the merchants wanted to shove down my throat. A few people were starting to catch on that the way things were working wasn't quite so great as they were made out to be, but whenever they said anything about it they were shouted down for being negative. And who would argue against profits and progress except malcontents and socialists? Most people went on yapping about the importance of a renewed entrepreneurial spirit, even though there wasn't much left to be entrepreneurial about. The best forests were gone, like I said, the big game stocks were diminished in the few areas where tourists might want to hunt, and it was too rough and too cold for other kinds of tourists.

Around that time I started thinking a lot about the old cave. Then I started going out there. Most of the equipment had been chewed by mice and rabbits, the metal corroded with rust. But slowly, and without much conscious thought of what I was doing, I replaced and improved most of it. The governments were talking about the need for austerity, which meant that they were doing less reforestation than ever, and they were giving the big corporations tax breaks so they could haul their profits back to the U.S. and Europe unmolested. On the other side of it they were hiring more police and setting up teams of investigators to harass people about their unemployment insurance and welfare—even though there were no jobs to be had and no way for most people to get off welfare. And the governments were mainly interested in buying bigger and better weapons, keeping the arms manufacturers rich. The country was going bankrupt, slowly but surely.

After a year or two of that I was dead broke, and when I realized I wasn't going to get work anywhere, I moved into the cave. The town had grown too violent for me, the streets swept alternately by gangs of the hungry unemployed and the police. One was as dangerous as the other. On the outskirts of town, in the suburbs, those who still had jobs spent their money in the shopping centres, watched television from Atlanta and places like that on their satellite dishes, and alternately patrolled their neighbourhoods as vigilantes or improved the electronic security systems in their fenced homes. It seemed like people were either scared or angry all the time, one or the other, and it meant that nobody was seeing things clearly, and nobody was talking to anyone. So, I got out.

I got out because it was over, not because I was one of those survivalists you hear about. I ran into some of those shitheads, and they weren't any different from the people who screwed up this place. They just wanted some place to shoot off their guns and act like there was a war on, and you could see, just under

204

the skin, that they really wanted to kill somebody. A lot of people, through history, seem to have thought like that. But only idiots and small boys can play at that game for very long. At some point you either grow up or you go completely crazy. So the survivalists didn't hang around these parts very long. I guess they all went back to California where you don't have to put up with cold winters and real survival problems.

Down at the mouth of the creek that ran out of the lake I built some weirs and caught trout, and I hunted the moose and deer that were proliferating in the logged-over forests. The poor people tried to hunt them too, but they usually hunted in packs, without much success. It was as if they'd become too demoralized to concentrate, and the animals easily avoided their clumsy and over-mechanized forays. You can't do much of anything with a gang except look for other gangs to fight with, and more often than not the hunters ended up shooting at other hunters.

Things got worse and worse. It wasn't because the people in charge went crazy. It was because everybody, the poor people and the entrepreneurs and the police, all tried to keep on doing what they'd been doing since the first days white people came here. They'd never paid attention to the things around them, just worked things over for what could be gained from them. And in the end, there were only other people to work over.

●

I've been living in the cave for five months now, all winter. I haven't a clue what's going on in town, and I don't really care to know. A while back, though, I discovered that I'm not alone. I was scouting the rear passages of the cave near the spring, and I found a network of new caves, all of them huge, and with a welcome addition. The walls were impregnated with a luminous substance that allows me to see without artificial light. I don't know how it works, but its a blessing, since my batteries were about dead when I found them, and I don't much relish the idea of going outside.

Anyway, in one of the caves I found about a dozen grizzlies. They were hibernating when I stumbled onto them. I've never

205

heard of so many of them being in one place at the same time. They began to wake up a couple of months back, and pretty soon they were actively roaming through the caves, feeding on the lichen that grows on the walls. At first I gave them a wide berth, expecting them to be irritable the way they are when they come out of hibernation. But these ones weren't starving, and as my own supplies have dwindled, I've begun to follow their example by eating the lichen myself. The lichens aren't the tastiest food I've ever eaten, but they seem to provide adequate nutrition. And by observing the grizzlies, I've begun to understand them, their grunts and snuffles and roars. They ignore me, and lately I've been able to pass within a dozen feet of them without their showing alarm or an inclination to attack. For all of us, it is live and let live. This afternoon, if that's what it is, a young male followed me for more than an hour, stopping wherever I stopped, and watching everything I did with apparent curiosity. As the day wore on he closed the distance between us until he was no more than a few feet behind me.

Maybe one of these days I'll go outside the cave again, and then again, maybe I won't. There's someone else in these caves besides the grizzlies and me—someone or something. Lately I've been catching glimpses of it. It's an old, decrepit, white-haired creature who won't let me come near. Or maybe I don't try very hard.

Sometimes in the night I hear the creature singing. But it's never very long before the song becomes a crazy kind of howling, and that isn't how I want to remember my own species. Other times, the song sinks to a low moan that disturbs the grizzlies, and is soon drowned out by their roars as they rush through the corridors between caves in the luminous half light. I think they're hunting the creature down.